WINGS OF AN ANGEL

Novelette

Written by

Isobel Rondeau

Copyright © 2021 Isobel Rondeau

All rights reserved. No portion of this book may be reproduced in any form without permission from the publisher, except as permitted by U.S. copyright law.

Dedication

For Mark who always has my back

Shawn and Alissa who believe I can do anything I set my mind to

Tina who pushes me beyond my limits and has unwavering confidence

in me

In loving memory of Jonathan, Tyler and Dillon

PROLOGUE

I wait watching

My body unceremoniously tossed like garbage into the hole

Silently I rage

I can see, hear, smell, taste and feel my life as it should have been

They will pay, they have to pay

It's how life is, its karma

Silently I cry and watch as my wings unfurl

Ready to fly away

Ready to join Creator

Wait…I'm not ready

I'm NOT ready.

CHAPTER ONE

Bolting awake, the remnants of screams lingering in my brain, I take a deep breath and looked around my spacious room. The blinds are closed to the early morning daylight trying to sneak in around the edges. Taking a long relaxing breath I close my eyes trying to picture the girl in my dream, like little whips of clarity I get flashes of images, her long, long dark hair, brown eyes riddled with pain, mouth open in a silent scream. Wondering how or what she was trying to say to me across the vastness of our universe. The thin veil of the afterlife, open to me on many occasions, closed its doors with a snap. Sighing, I open my eyes and sit up in bed, wearily rubbing my eyes and running a hand through my sleep tossed hair. Glancing over at my night table I reach for my phone, I see the early hour and groan, it is very early, to early to get out of bed, but knowing I will not be able to sleep again, I slip my feet into my soft slippers. I might as well get on with my day. Heading across the room my leather slippers making a whisper noise on the thick blue carpet. The 1900 square foot elegant apartment is silent so early in the day. Heading to the kitchen I make a strong coffee. The gleaming white marble kitchen hurts my eyes, blindly grabbing a cup I add in a heaping spoonful of sugar and have my first sip, ahhh the taste of bitter coffee with a sweet aftertaste. Best part of my day. Walking out to the patio, I wonder at the beautiful colours coming from the east, enjoy every precious

CHAPTER ONE

moment as it will never happen twice. Smiling, I remember a time with my dear friend and Elder, John Runningwater. Sipping my now cooled coffee, I look around and take in the beautiful scenery available to me from the top floor, the penthouse. There are plenty of trees and green grass across from me at the park, there are a couple of joggers, some street people, the early morning traffic is yet to be clogged and noisy with horns honking and people gesturing to each other in their hurry to get to their respective offices. Yellow cabs drive slowly by waiting for their radios to let them know their first pickup of the day. Closing my eyes I listen to the birds calling to each other far below, so peaceful. A flicker, a childhood memory, running barefoot through the forest, laughter on my lips, older boys whooping in delight, the sunlight filtering through the thick branches. The crunch of pine needles underfoot. Sighing, it was a long time ago, sometimes it feels like a lifetime or two.

Heading back inside, I return to my gleaming bright kitchen, place the empty coffee mug on the counter, I tell myself I will make time today to sit and enjoy a cup later on. First a shower, then breakfast and into the office I go, wondering what type of horrors I will have to face today. The hot water spraying all the negative thoughts clinging to me from the night, swirl down

CHAPTER ONE

the drain and I am happy to let them go. I quickly clean up, dry off and grab my usual outfit from the closet to dress for 'work'. Dark blue jeans and a soft cotton button up white shirt.

First, to call Detective Reynolds, stern, rule abiding and a little uptight, maybe she just doesn't feel comfortable around me.

"Hello, my name is Mark Whitestone, I'm calling to speak to Detective Reynolds. Yes, I will hold". I wait, listening to tinny country music playing on the phone.

"Detective Reynolds here Mr. Whitestone, we have a busy day, five new cases, meet me at Casey's Diner I need to try get something into my stomach that I just emptied after reading the first case." After a quick pause to catch her breath the detective ends our call with, "see you in 15 minutes, don't be late"

I guess my day has officially begun. Hanging up the phone, I briefly wonder if she would even listen if I said I was busy and couldn't meet her today. Probably not. Replaying her one sided conversation, I cringed at what five cases would mean for me. No more lazy mornings, I had to help families

CHAPTER ONE

who had missing people, it was my gift to them, to bring closure, to let them try to move on with a gaping hole in their family. In my years of working with the police force I had only missed one person, she still haunted me on occasion. Grabbing my wallet, keys and sunglasses I make my way to the garage. Glancing at the vehicles sitting like little soldiers, waiting their turn on the road, I smile as I spot the one who will take me around today. The Mercedes. The ride is quick, smooth and relaxing. Just what I need to start my day.

Pulling in to the diner parking lot I easily find a spot to park my Mercedes Benz Maybach Exelero, my one weakness with money, my vehicles. The white interior calmed me, I could meditate in the quiet, the leather soothing my senses, listening to smooth drumming from my home on the speakers. The lot was almost empty save for a few modest suv type cars. I noticed Detective Reynolds vehicle immediately, boring, black, sedan. Good thing she wasn't an undercover cop, I think to myself as I walk by it.

Entering the diner I notice the smell first, the sweet smell of fresh baking, cinnamon buns fresh from the oven, the tangy sweetness of warm syrup. My

CHAPTER ONE

mouth waters as I realize I only had one cup of coffee this morning. Eager to eat I glance around and find Detective Vivian Reynolds in the back booth, she looks a little green. My stomach drops, maybe food isn't the answer right now. Her long dark hair tied back in a no nonsense bun, her head bowed, she looks like she is praying. Quickly making my way to her, I slide into the booth, the cold red leather like silk on my back side. Making eye contact with Detective Reynolds I reach for the menu, asking if she has ordered anything. She shakes her head in the negative and her green eyes look down to the white formica table top. The young waitress comes over and I ask for two ice waters and then order fresh fruit, yogurt and granola, two teas and two cinnamon buns. As she walks away to place our order I look again at the detective, if we are going to be working so closely I should know her first name. The bags under her eyes clearly suggest a tough morning and possibly a rough night as well. Her long lashes lay on her pale cheeks, mouth drawn tight. The all black suit she wore looked rumpled and it wasn't even noon.

"Rough day?" I ask gently

"One of the roughest" she sighed.

CHAPTER ONE

Without raising her eyes, she pulls a file from her briefcase and slides it across the table to me. Reaching for it my hand stops and hovers just above the cream coloured folder. I hesitate to touch it just yet.

"Let's just talk before I open this up. That ok with you?" I ask her.

Finally she looks at me, eye to eye, and nods okay. I move my hands together without touching the file folder and clasp them in front of me on the table. I assume she cannot converse just yet so I start.

"I can see your shaken by what is in the file, lets start with you telling me your name, Detective Reynolds is quite a mouthful and if we are going to be working together I need more info about you". Hopefully she can answer that simple question without falling apart.

She looks up and a hint of a smile graces her lips,

CHAPTER ONE

"Detective Reynolds is actually shorter than my name…Vivienne Magdalaine Angelique Reynolds, its French, my parents were very traditional. But you can call me Ren or Viv, I answer to both. However in any reports you must refer to me as Detective Reynolds as well as at any crime scenes we may have to attend."

Smiling at her answer I easily reply,"Well I will try both those names out and see which one fits you best, Viv. I notice you have no wedding ring, I also know officers don't always wear their rings, so are you married or common law and do you have any children?" I had to know if she would be distracted by family in the event we were on a dangerous call somewhere. Then to correct myself, I admit that I actually just want to know because she is an enigma to me, her tenderness at war with her tough cop attitude. I am curious that's all, I smartly tell myself.

"Not married, no boyfriend or significant other, unless you count the job. No children as of yet and honestly I am not sure I would like to bring any into the world we live in today." She glances again at the folder on the table.

CHAPTER ONE

Troubled eyes look up at me and she asks the same questions, "should I call you Mark or Whitestone? And spouse or children?"

"Mark is just fine, unless we are with your superiors, then you can call me Mr. Whitestone" I smile to her.

She smiles and shakes her head. "Mark then, and I am probably not going to call you Mr. anything"

Liking her attitude, I answer her other question, "no spouse for me and no children so far, although I think about them from time to time, I might like to have a boy I could hunt and fish with, or a girl who would sew like my mother and grandmother."

Just then our water and teas arrive, the waitress smiles at me, far to young to smile like that at customers, I thank her and turn back to Viv.

"How long have you been a Detective?" I ask

CHAPTER ONE

Looking a bit more relaxed Viv pours and stirs some honey into her tea and looks out the booth window.

Sitting up a bit straighter she says, "I started the Police Academy right out of high school, finished training in the top three of my class. That was tough. I was an officer for five years, I was trained in Vancouver, the toughest streets in Canada. I learned a lot there. When a position came up in rural Alberta I had to go. I had been trained about burn out and didn't want to have that happen to me right off the bat. I have finished several Psychology courses and am trained in PTSD, Post Traumatic Stress Disorder. I handled many domestic abuse cases and after a few years my superior noticed my attention to detail and the follow through I had with some of the victims. He appreciated it and talked me into trying to pass the exam for the Alberta Law Enforcement Response Team (Alert) I am now a Senior Detective within this branch. I work all over Alberta but am stationed in Edmonton. I thought I could try to make a difference in the communities I attended. Had wanted to educate the men and women I came in contact with, and their children. Violence is never the answer. However, it seems some days what I do just isn't enough."

CHAPTER ONE

Her sigh on the last sentence, tugged at me. Glancing up I saw the waitress carrying our food towards us. Moving my glass of water and tea I smiled to the girl as she placed our food on the table. Thanking her and assured her that we needed nothing more. She walked away. Looking back to Viv I motioned that she should start filling her plate with whatever she needed. Taking the tongs she placed two strawberry slices and a slice of melon and then added a spoonful of vanilla greek yogurt then she placed one of the cinnamon buns on the side of her plate. Hoping she finished that and had more I just took one of the buns and tasted. It was better than it smelled. Almost heavenly. The dough crisp yet melted in my mouth. A low moan escaped me as I swallowed. My eyes closed I hear her laugh, enjoying the moment for one second longer, I open my eyes to see her looking at me in wonder.

"The best taste in the world is fresh cinnamon buns" I smile at her.

CHAPTER ONE

I notice she has pushed her yogurt around on her plate, the three pieces of fruit still there. Not a single bite out of the bun. Gently I take her bun and tear a small bite off, I put it to her mouth and say, "try it, its really delicious."

She actually opens her mouth and takes the small taste, "thank you." She says.

I can see the thoughts rolling around her head, some indecision at what she has just done. We hardly know each other. I continue eating as if what just transpired was normal and not me trying to get the Detective to eat. Quietly we eat our meal, well I eat a meal, Viv mostly just pushes her food around till its mush on her plate. At least she drinks the tea and water. I notice the colour return to her face and her breathing become more regular. I have managed to relax her and now maybe she is ready to talk about the case in a more professional manner. As I finish my fruit and motion the waitress for more tea I glance at the folder. Hesitant to break the silence I reach a hand over to the folder, the detective immediately tenses up.

CHAPTER ONE

I look at her and say, "I just want to read it, if I have questions or comments I will let you know."

She nods her head and sips on her tea. Watching me expectantly.

Touching my hand to the folder, my vision blurs, I take a deep breath, closing my eyes I try to relax. A red haired boy, short hair, dimples, eyes to big and blue to belong to his face, I hear a faint giggle.

"I'm here" he whispers to me.

"Go away" he shouts as a singsong voice interrupts
"are you here to help me go home?" The melodic voice asks me.

Again the voice changes, "I want my mommy."
Another cries.
Others try to chime in but I mentally sort them out, like a rainbow each voice has a hue, taking a breath I slowly tell each of them that I want to help

CHAPTER ONE

but they need to listen to me. Quieting down I concentrate on the little red haired boy.

"Hello, my name is Mark. Do you need my help?" I quietly think these thoughts.

He answers almost immediately "I want out, and I want to go home, everyone is bossy here. I miss my big sister, and my mom and daddy." His voice wavers a little bit on the last words.

Before he can start crying I ask the most important question, "Do you know where you are?"

"I don't know, but its dark and there's a scary man who watches me, he has a black hat, I don't like him" he pouts.

Again, I try to get a location or some kind of landmark from him, "are you by the water? Are there buildings by you? Do you hear vehicles driving by?"

CHAPTER ONE

"I don't know" he answers.

Suddenly he's gone along with all the rest of them. Blinking my eyes I cringe at the bright light coming in the windows, and realize I am still sitting in the booth with Detective Reynolds. My hand on the closed folder. The detective looks at me with questions in her eyes.

"Are you going to open it?" She asks

"Of course" I reply as I mentally clear the clutter in my mind.

I gently pull the folder in front of me. Opening it up I am forced to read the statistics of the child who I was just talking to. His name is Tyler and he has been missing for thirty eight days. Three feet tall, auburn hair, blue eyes, three years old. My heart hurts knowing that the family will not hold their little boy again, his sister won't get to grow up playing soccer in the yard with her little brother. No first dates, no prom night, no wedding, no children, or grandchildren. Just nothing. Gone like he never existed. Reading on I take in the crime scene photos, blood, spattered on yellowed wallpaper, ripped

CHAPTER ONE

clothes, how could things like this happen to a three year old. Sighing I close my eyes and pray to Creator that these souls are found and returned home for

proper grieving with their families. I turn the page and read the next victim case file.

Female, age 7, missing 108 days, camping site pictures where she was taken from, same M.O. Blood spatter, torn clothes.

I hear her singsong voice, "will you help me get home, I need to tell my mommy that I love her, I need to hug her and tell her I will be ok"

Shaking my head, I try to answer her, but it doesn't always work both ways.

Next file, female, age 5, missing 148 days, same M.O.
Next file, male, age 5, missing 300 days same M.O.
Last file, female, age 2, missing 456 days same M.O.

The whimpers echo in my brain, trying to drown them out I hum a little tune Elder John gave me. Slowly they disappear and I am left with wet lashes

CHAPTER ONE

and a breaking heart. I need a minute to calm down. I take a sip of cool water and look at the detective. She has her eyes on me, business eyes.

"Well," she says "ready to work?"

"I am not sure about taking on this case," I whisper to the detective I have a journey that needs to be completed. This case might be the one that is to big. "Give me 48 hours, if I get things sorted before that, I will call the station."

Nodding slightly, I signal to the waitress for our check. After paying and leaving a generous tip, we walk outside into the sunlight. The detective and I make a time to meet up later on in the week and I watch the detective elegantly slide into her non descript, boring, black car and drive away.

Sighing, I look at my car, sparkling in the bright sunlight. I have to complete my journey, it's the only way to bring closure, to heal, to help, to begin living.

Sliding into the cool interior, I adjust my sunglasses. Take a breath I hold and release slowly. It's going to be ok, I just have to deal with the horror of

CHAPTER ONE

my past. Easy. It's only taken me years to get this far. 48 hours. I have a deadline. Easing out into traffic I head home.

CHAPTER TWO

Hastily packing an overnight bag, I make sure my apartment is secure and I jump into my black Range Rover. Quickly I drive down the highway, music blaring, I drown out any thoughts trying to sneak in. Soon the buildings fade and yellow Canola and green and golden hayfields fill my vision for miles. The land looks like a giant patchwork quilt. I smile grateful to be alive and able to see the wonderful colour and know the fields will bring food to our communities. It's beautiful this big country that I live in. I glimpse a long haired warrior wearing leather leggings with paint on his face, seated on a big, spotted, buckskin brown stallion, running across a lush green field. They stop and turn to look at me, meeting my eyes. Then they disappear. Just gone. I take a look at the nav system, almost there. The shiver in my soul makes me aware of how far I am going back. But I have to finish this journey, Elder John is expecting me to.

This is the second time I have been down this road, literally and figuratively. So many years ago I couldn't complete the mission I had set, this time I have more tools in my tool kit. The teachings from Elder John would help and guide me. I had learned the hard way not to listen to the visions, or to trust them completely. Thinking back to Elder John I smile,

CHAPTER TWO

he was a tough old bird. Shoulders stooped from a life of hard labour, his smiling, brown eyes. The hint of laughter in every spoken word. Hours and hours we spent together, walking the land and harvesting medicines. Learning to respect the land and giving thanks for all we had. I went from being an adult to a child again, learning everything I could. I would cherish every minute we had gotten to be together. I vividly recall the day he passed into the other plane. His final journey. I had just woken up and saw him at the foot of my bed, his brown eyes had sadness in them. I had thought that was weird as he was always smiling and happy. I heard his voice but he didn't seem to move his mouth and my groggy head understood before my eyes could. He said to be good and heal my heart and then he said I was the closest thing to family he had had in many years and thanked me for walking beside him for as long as I could. He said goodbye for now and he would see me soon enough. Saddened by his loss, I closed my eyes and said a thank you for the precious time we got to spend together.

Sighing, I think back to my last trip, going over all the little mistakes.

FIVE YEARS AGO:

CHAPTER TWO

The day I returned to the field it was hot, muggy and still. Blue skies as far as you could see. The laughter and squeals from children echoed across the green fields. The lone merry go round still in the morning sunlight. My age weary eyes looked in all directions, first to the Heavens above, then right to left scanning the horizon for signs of mercy, finally my head hung down and I looked at the earth. My heart wondering again after years of conflict and doubts, how, how on earth had Creator allowed the tragedy to happen. I was so angry at all the injustices that had happened to so many families. Lifting my head I looked at the building in front of me, the stones crumbling, windows smashed out of the frames, graffiti spray painted across the fading red bricks. Heart heavy I started forward only to be stopped in my tracks by a vision, a little girl walking on the roof, her sparkling white shoes pinching her toes because they were to small, her long chestnut hair tied tightly back in a ponytail with a white ribbon wrapped around the elastic. Her dress was long, to her ankles and the cloth itched her waist where the dress was held tightly to her small waist with a long black belt. She looked towards me and her mouth opened as if she wanted to talk to me, instead she turned and ran

CHAPTER TWO

towards the end of the roof. My breath caught as I watched her jump. The vision cleared, my heart racing, I swiped at the tears that had gathered in the corners of my eyes. I looked up towards the empty roof, nothing but clear blue sky. I turned on my heel and drove away without a glance back.

PRESENT DAY:

For as long as I could remember I had had the visions. Sometimes they were brief glimpses, sometimes they were whole life stories in the span of an instant. My grandmother had said I was special, gifted by the Creator to help others, guide them in their times of turmoil and grief. Until I was about seven, I believed her.

Our community was happy to feed me when I came around to visit them, I had plenty of friends and cousins in the small community. Up to that point my life was pretty average, filled with laughter and stories, fishing and feeding the community was a part of my daily chore. I didn't think of it as a chore but something that just was. Helping my older

CHAPTER TWO

cousins clean and carry the fish to my mother and aunties, then they would scale and cook the fish. I remember

the beautiful art my mother made with the fish scales, the colours dancing in the sunlight. Walking along the dusty road delivering fish to the Elders in our community was something I cherished, I always came away with a story or a new lesson on being kind, helping others and sharing what we had. I thought they were ancient with their long white hair tied back with leather, I especially loved it when they would play music for me and the others when they saw us walking up the path with our packs slung over our shoulders. A drum beating, a voice singing a song of thanks, happy eyes and welcoming arms greeting us at every stop.

The carefree days of living a simple life, and in the blink of an eye it was gone. Everything had been ripped away from me in one fall day. I remember the leaves were changing on the trees, we had picked as many berries as we could and had canned them to eat throughout the winter months. My stomach was full as my cousins and I had eaten as many as we had picked, my tiny fingers were stained a purple colour. I was anxiously waiting for every chore to be complete so we could play a game of hide and seek before twilight. I heard the cries before the white van

CHAPTER TWO

came to our house, long mourning cries, it sounded like the wolves we heard cry during the winter when they were hungry. My grandmother ran out of the house and scooped me up and the others ran behind her as she yelled for them to hurry hurry hurry. I started crying, I hadn't seen Nohkom act this way before. Before we could get to the forest the white van had stopped in front of us. My Nohkom screamed at the older boys to run into the forest and hide until someone came to get them. The boys scattered but my Nohkom held me tightly to her chest. The people had gotten out of the van by then and a couple tried to go into the forest to find my cousins. But one man, the driver, came to my Nohkom and told her to let me go. She refused and I held her tightly around her neck crying softly into her soft white hair, she smelled like pine cones. She kept repeating to me that she loved me and everything would be alright. The man told her to stop speaking gibberish. By then one of the people had come back with one of my older cousins, he was quietly weeping but didn't fight it when he was put into the white van. My Nohkom was distracted by the scene and the man beside her hastily pulled me from her arms. She tried to grab me back but someone was holding her arms down by her sides. The man put me in the white van without saying a word to

CHAPTER TWO

me or my Nohkom. And then we were driving away from the only home I had ever known. My life changed that instant.

CHAPTER THREE

Slowly relearning about my heritage had been painful, emotional and draining. Still, as I had learned, the path is a long one to forgiveness. The trip I had taken to come to this hellish nightmare of a memory was a vital piece of my journey towards forgiveness. Part of healing, keeping sober and helping others. Forgiveness, the word is easy, the deed is harder. Glimpsing the hill, the long driveway and the towering red roof peeking over the maple trees, my stomach turns a little queasy. This time I will complete the mission, I have had five years to prepare myself. I need to do this in order to move on with my life. To honour a promise to my friend, my mentor, my business partner and I reluctantly admit, to myself.

Parking my suv I climb out and gravel crunches beneath my shoes. I hesitate to look up, scared to see the little girl in white. I haven't heard any voices, no whispers in my ears, but I am actually frozen in spot, like a deer in headlights. Closing my eyes, I feel the sun warm my face, I take a deep breath keeping the door firmly closed to any wayward thoughts, I slowly let it out and open my eyes. My heartbeat slow and steady. I look toward the roof and there's nothing, just clear blue sky. Closing and locking the car door I start towards the crumbling steps, easier now, I am

CHAPTER THREE

more confident in myself and my abilities to put to rest my tormentors. After all I had made a promise.

As I walk up the crumbling stairs, I think how small they are, only seven steps up. My hand reaches to the end of my long braided hair, clutching the wiry thickness and finding the leather tie. Closing my eyes I take a deep cleansing breath and count to three and slowly release it. In with the good, out with the bad. I haven't been able to walk back to this place, the place I had died emotionally. The stone walls of the building had stifled me. Oh how I had missed the freedom of the forest, the swift running water where we fished, the tiny boarded houses and strong teepees that housed us all. Touching the rusted brass of the door knob, I was shocked with another vision.

I was a little boy, limp with exhaustion from crying silently in the white van. I was starting up the cold red brick steps to the huge building. It was like nothing I had ever seen before. I missed our little house and my Nohkom's teepee. Three heads hovered high above me, white haired, glasses, frowning, a look I had not seen in my life up to that point. I was

CHAPTER THREE

scared, I missed my Nohkom. They took turns talking to me in a language I hardly understood. As two turned away the third one grabbed me by my slender shoulder and spat in my face. I was crying harder now, understanding that this was not a nice place. I tried to run from him but he held my shirt and dragged me inside. Then I remember the darkness.

Shaking my head, my vision cleared, I had to get control or I would never make it through this journey. Breathing raggedly I hummed the tune Elder John had taught me and remembered to breathe slowly. I calmed down and continued forward.

Turning the handle, I pushed open the door. It was squeaky and made a loud noise, harsh to my ears. Even though the sun was shining outside and the windows were smashed, the light that entered the building was dark and little dust motes floated in the air when the door opened. Haltingly I entered, keeping the door open behind me, I tested the floor to make sure I wouldn't crash through to the basement. The building, made of stone, was intact inside. I had hoped it would be crumbling and unsafe to enter. Stepping one foot in front of the other I entered the

CHAPTER THREE

cafeteria, empty but for the echo of tin plates being placed in the bin, the spoons scraping off the moldy, worm infested food. At the time, I didn't know why but none of us had forks or knives, later on I learned why. Savages didn't need utensils, didn't know what to do with them. I think the nuns were scared we would have used the utensils to scalp them as they slept. Like I had any intention of doing that at seven years old. Shaking my head and trying to see the building as the place it was, a jail, a torture chamber, an evil place. I didn't go to the kitchen, I went back to the main room and entered another doorway, the school room. It use to be full of books and writing tools. The books were mostly Bibles. There were drawers full of pencils and rulers. The Sisters were never, ever short of rulers. The dark room, now empty, had once had long tables where we were suppose to study the Bibles under the watchful eyes of the nuns. They quietly walked up and down the space in between the tables. Slapping the rulers in their hands making loud distracting sounds, only to whack you with the ruler if you dared to raise your eyes or your head from the reading of God's book. After being in this place for years I had finally forgotten about my Creator, and started thinking there was only God and his Bible. The nuns and priests had beaten my religion, my way of life out

CHAPTER THREE

of me. For every mistake I had made, I frantically prayed for God's forgiveness, and after many years and many many mistakes I had come to realize that I needed no forgiveness from my Creator as he loved and cherished all creation for what they were.

As the scenery changed, my mind closed the memories with a gentle nudge. After that one visit five years ago, my life had changed. I had wanted to stop the visions, I drank a lot to drown out the voices. I thought returning to the place I hated most in the world would transform me. Make me whole or whatever. But it hadn't. I had returned home feeling like what little life I had left was just gone. I had questions, who was the little girl on the roof, what had happened to the nuns who were in charge, and unable to face those questions, I decided I had to drown my sorrows or shut the door on it all and start anew. After a rough alcohol filled week, I looked in my cracked bathroom mirror, the broken nose, bruised face, unkempt and dirty and I knew I had to shut the door. With a slam. I went through my tiny apartment, threw away anything that had association with alcohol. I cleaned and it sparkled, a little diamond in the rough, just like me. I went to AA meetings and learned strategies, it helped. I got a job, it

CHAPTER THREE

kept my mind off of drinking, it's where I met Elder John. Our friendship was almost perfect, a blending of souls. He was like the big brother that I never got to grow up with. He always had a ready story, an antidote and a ready smile, eager to help all who crossed his path. He asked for my help with a few cases he was working on with the police department. At first I was reluctant, I had never really had a good relationship with the local authorities. But, after a couple positive case file closures and meeting a couple officers who had great attitudes, John had asked if I wanted to go into business with him. On a consulting basis. There was a movement in the police force to improve their image with the Indigenous communities across Canada and Elder John wanted to help bridge that gap. I didn't have to think long about it. The job I had was a dead end, this was an opportunity, and I would get to work and get paid to be with Elder John. I knew he would be a lifelong friend and mentor. The answer was an easy yes.

CHAPTER FOUR

My memories fading again I look towards the stairs that led up, "the first step is always the hardest" I can hear Elder John whisper to me.

I test my weight on the bottom stair. It holds and so I hesitantly place another foot on the next one. I look towards the top, noticing the faded grooves in the handrails, the stairs and the curling piece of faded rug at the top. Breathing in and holding for two counts I breathe slowly out. Climbing higher I start getting dizzy but I hold on and climb to the top. Like my feet know where to go without me giving direction, I start to the left, the boys rooms. The carpet is crusty under my shoes, the crunch sounding like cannons in the quiet building. There are five missing doors on this side of the building, one was a washroom. The wash basins had all been smashed to bits, I didn't enter the room but I imagined the toilets were all smashed as well. Next to this room was the baby boy room, my rooms. The new boys who were under ten stayed here. The metal bunks were still lined up against the walls but the skinny mattresses, yellow with pee stains, were all gone. I flick the light switch knowing it won't work, emotions I can't describe building inside me. Wanting to let the feelings out and work through them, I try to sort them one by one. It is hard work

CHAPTER FOUR

to single out an emotion, like separating the colours of a rainbow. Walking to the window, this one had stayed intact for all these years, I look down at the brown dead grass and the overgrown mound of dirt. My head spins with memories. Catching a glimpse of white in my peripheral vision I turn my head, the faint rustle of fabric on the floor, I thought I saw white at the edge of the doorway. Curiosity clutching my heart, I wondered who else had come to this place, were their memories and nightmares made of the same frighteningly vivid stories? Was it the little brown haired girl from years ago? Without much hesitation I move quickly towards the door, leaving my boyhood memories behind.

Looking down the corridor I see it's empty. Thinking the person went into another room, I quietly call out, "hello?" And receive no answer.

Walking quickly, I glance in every doorway, nobody anywhere, I must have just thought I saw something. My body involuntary gives a little shudder and my arms get goosebumps. I hear a soft sob. Was it imaginary, in my head, I sort the sound, and know it isn't in my head. Someone else is in the building with me. I take out my phone and turn on the flashlight,

CHAPTER FOUR

there are no footprints on the cement floor. There is no movement of air in the hot hallway, that seems a little weird considering all or most of the windows have been broken out of the window panes. Again I hear a whisper of a sound coming from the floor below me. I turn and head back towards the staircase. Curiosity making me hurry. Reaching the bottom of the stairs I turn towards the kitchen area.

In the kitchen area I see a beautiful lady dressed in blue, no white on her dress, stirring something in a bowl. Her long gloriously white hair is tightly braided and hangs down her back, the end tied tightly with a piece of leather. She turns her head towards me as I cross the threshold into the kitchen, her lips turn upwards in a welcoming smile, brown eyes sparkling.

"Hello" she greets me in a musical voice. "I didn't know when to expect you. Elder John Runningwater has told me so much about you, I feel like we are family already."

"Hello" I answer automatically

CHAPTER FOUR

"I am making bannock, would you care to join me for some when it is ready?" She asks

"Thank you, yes, I would." Wondering who she is, I say, "you knew John then. I am sorry but he has not mentioned you to me."

Softly I also let her know that John Runningwater has recently left this earth.

"Oh I know about that," she says smiling, "we have been friends since we were just new, he was like a father to me for many years."

Briefly I try to remember the people who had attended the service for Elder John and I cannot remember seeing her there.

I watch as she deftly folds the bread dough gently in the pan and sets it aside. Wiping her hands on a tea towel tucked into the belt at her waist. Turning her back to me she adjusts the knobs on the oven. She reminds

CHAPTER FOUR

me of my grandmother, her sway when walking, the tilt of her head right before she talks.

"So Mark," she starts, "my name is Roseanne"

I quickly look closer at her, that is my grandmothers name, my Nohkom, whom I have not seen since I was seven years old. Although this lady could not be her, age wise it just wasn't possible. This Roseanne was younger than me, however, I knew not to close off any possibilities.

"That is a beautiful name," I respond softly "my grandmothers name is Roseanne." I tell her.

"Yes" she replies warmly with a smile on her lips, "I know your grandmother, she is the most beautiful lady, strong, smart and so kind."

"How did you know her?" I ask

CHAPTER FOUR

Hearing the oven ding, letting her know the temperature was set, Roseanne gently carried the pan to the oven and put it inside, setting the timer for 22 minutes. The exact time my grandmother also cooked her bannock.

Trying to temper my anxiety, I ask again, "when did you meet my grandmother?"

Roseanne looks over her shoulder like she hears something. I notice Roseanne's frown before she smiles and looks at me again.

"I am sorry but I need to attend to something in the other room, would you remove the bread from the oven when the timer buzzes. Please" she waits for my answer.

Nodding my head affirmative, I wonder what she heard to make her have to leave.

"Do you need any help" I ask her

CHAPTER FOUR

"I will be back as soon as I can" she answers,

and then is out the doorway quickly before I can ask any further questions. I notice the smell of pine cones as she leaves.

Feeling a bit thirsty in the hot kitchen I go to the cupboards to look for a glass and find nothing but dust. I turn to the fridge hoping there is a cold bottle of water in there. The fridge is sparkling clean, weird. Whoever could live in this place, I wonder with a shudder. Inside the fridge is a bottle of water, unopened, and some butter and a jar of chokecherry jam. Just like I use to have

as a child. Taking the bottle out and closing the door I see little dust swirls from the sunlight beams, I open and drink deeply, the water feels wonderful on my parched throat. Going to the window over the sink I notice the dead bugs on the sill, the dust clinging to the cracked pane.

I smell the bannock cooking, a quick flash of my grandmothers teepee, smoky and warm, smelling of cooked fish and fresh bannock. The glimpse is so fast but I hear my grandmother laugh and almost feel the

CHAPTER FOUR

warmth of her arms as she wraps me in a hug. I hear the oven timer ring and then my vision clears and I look around.

Still in the dusty kitchen I walk to the oven to check the bannock. Opening the oven door I see that its empty, the oven cold and dirty. My head spinning I go to the fridge, the door hangs crookedly on the rusted hinges. Opening the heavy door I notice the heavy layer of grime. No jar of jam, no butter and not clean like it was just minutes ago. I wonder how my visions can be coming so often, the stress of being here? Why are they so vivid in this horrible place? Closing my eyes I ask Creator to guide me safely and keep me on the trail of forgiveness and truth. Breathing softly and evenly I open my eyes and begin again. Leaving the kitchen I enter the long hallway remembering the gleaming wood floors. Looking at my hands I remember the peeling skin I had endured as a child, the lye used to rub the floors clean, how we had also had the lye used on us for soap, to clean away our sins the nuns had said. I was never sure if my sins had been cleansed but I started to pray to God when it was my turn to get washed. To hurry and wash my sins away so I could get out of the scalding hot water hoping it wasn't sister Sara who was

CHAPTER FOUR

washing us that day. She had mean eyes, and pinching fingers, she always had to check my private parts to make sure they were clean.

Another vision popped into my head taking me back to those horrible years.

Sister Sara drying me harshly with a white towel then making me stand upright while she fondled my privates, her lips smiling when my little body betrayed me. I could hear her voice scold me for being so brazen and not having proper control of my body. The lesson she had to teach me for being so lazy. I had to spend what seemed like days in a cell in the basement, the dark room only lit when the door was opened. She would visit me and bring actual food, not the wormy stuff.

Half an orange or a small apple. Sometimes I got a mint or a piece of liquorice. Eventually I would look forward to seeing her and what treat she would bring me. I had effectively blocked out the pain she also brought with her, the Father, he didn't speak a word to me, he physically hurt me over and over. There was a stain on the mattress, it was what I

CHAPTER FOUR

looked at when he was there. Just pain and grunting. I went to the room downstairs every couple of weeks. It had taken me a while to notice others would go away for days at a time, sometimes they wouldn't ever come back. There were whispers among the children but no one was certain what had happened. I imagined they went back home to their families. I thought how lucky they were to be able to fish and play in the lush green forest again. However, the older boys said they weren't at their homes but that they were out of pain now. The older boys always had grass and dirt stains on their pants. Years later I would accidentally see them digging holes in the ground at the bottom of the hill where we were not allowed. I had thought they were gardening, and they had been sometimes but they were also digging shallow graves for the children who had not survived the basement room. The ones who never returned.

My vision cleared so I took a deep breath, hold, count and relax. Breathe in slowly and hold, breathe out slowly. I opened my eyes and thought about all the children who had been here, all the years of hurt and humiliation. How they had all been brainwashed to change their way of life. How they had all been used and abused by their "teachers" who

CHAPTER FOUR

could survive that turmoil how does one live a normal life after? I know a return to your home, your mother, father, other damaged siblings, aunties, uncles, grandmothers, grandfathers, was impossible. I had tried. After years of abuse, brainwashed to love your abusers, to follow the rules obediently or fear the consequences. To loathe your body and your mind. I had been taught and then made to shutter any conversations with the spirits my Nohkom told me were special. The Sisters told me they were demons who were after my soul and that the Father would cleanse me of their hold on my soul so that I would be able to enter the heavenly fathers gates when my life was over.

Like an open door after the floods another vision came into focus.

Sitting in the dining hall, not eating the moldy food set in front of me, my little stomach growling in protest. Taking little sips of dirty water to calm the noises. After dinner the nuns took me away. The Father who conducted the demon cleansing was new, he never looked in my eyes and when I had looked up towards him he quickly told me to look down at the floor. I obeyed quickly as I feared the consequence. There were white

CHAPTER FOUR

candles lit and I was on the alter in the chapel. I had a white cloth wrapped around my naked bony body it was cold and I shivered. I can still feel his cold hands folded on my head. He had a cup of water which he poured over my hair. His mumblings, the brush of his black robe on the stone chapel floor. I noticed another set of shoes and another black robe join him. There were two voices chanting together now, asking God to remove the demons from my body. The gentle way he removed the white cloth wrapped around me and the bite on my flesh as he whipped me with a leather belt. My scream was loud, as I had never been hit before. Pinched, slapped, abused but never struck except for the nuns rulers and that was nothing compared to this pain. He shushed me and resumed his chanting, asking for the demon to be gone from my body. Silently I cried, hoping the demons left me but wondering where they would go. The chanting went on for hours. The darkness when I almost passed out from the pain a welcome thought, but the Father seemed to know the limits from which I could be brought to and I never got to go into the darkness. Over and over the bite of the belt on my back, my legs, my buttocks. I could feel warm rivulets of blood run down my sides and along my legs. Little pools of red blood falling to the cold stone alter where I lay. Finally

CHAPTER FOUR

it was over, the pain was white hot on my skin but the chanting and the whipping had stopped. My body was limp with fatigue my face streaked with silent tears. My cries had stopped long before. The Father patted my head and claimed I was cured

of the demons and that I could repay my gratitude to him shortly. The nun who had witnessed the exorcism quietly put a salve on my body, I whimpered with pain as the cloth was lain over my legs. The Father told her to leave and he would see to the cleaning of the wounds, she quickly got to her feet and left the church. The Father locked the door behind her and came back to the alter, and he addressed me for the first time since the exorcism had started.

"Open your mouth lad" his voice was raspy, his breathing was fast and uneven like he had just run a long distance. He came around to stand in front of me, he put his hand in my hair and raised up my head. His robe parted and his private parts stood erect, "God knows you must repay us for ridding you of the demons in your soul" I gagged but he held his

CHAPTER FOUR

hands on my head until I stopped then guided me to pleasure him until he was finished. My body was beaten, my soul was broken, I became a puppet for all the Fathers to follow. Finally I succumbed to the darkness. I awoke in my bed, the light telling me it was long past time to arise but my body would not get up. I couldn't move my legs and my back seemed to be sticking to the sheets on my bed. I must have made a noise as a young nun came into the boys room with a bowl of water and some towels. She made a gagging noise as she pulled the blanket back from me. She never said a word to me other than to turn over. She gently cleansed my wounds and stated she was finished and pulled a clean dressing gown over my head. I didn't feel clean. I was sure I would never be clean again. The spirits or demons had finally left my body.

Again the vision cleared. I remember that I never had another vision from that day until many years later.

My eyes had watered but no tears fell from my eyes. Never again was I going to feel that helpless, never again would I give another person control over me and my body. I owned my own life I had to make my

CHAPTER FOUR

way and control in every aspect was my way. It was how I was able to awake every morning and sleep every night. Although I still had trouble with the nighttime sleeping from time to time I knew, after all these years that control in all aspects of my life was needed to hold the terrors of my past at bay. I had tried the therapists way, I thought I had tried but I couldn't bear to walk into that clinic. I would feel like a child every time the doors opened. I did have a few therapy sessions sitting under a large tree with the sun shining down on me. The therapist while trying hard to help was still the product of the "white" schooling system and I couldn't get past the thoughts that came into my head that this woman who only wanted to help me, could never imagine the horrors that I had endured. I only went to six or so sessions and other than bringing feelings of anger to the surface I felt nothing positive had come of these sessions.

As I stood there amid the dusty kitchen cupboards memories flashed by,

At 18 years of age, I was timid, I had been told what to wear, eat, say, how to act, physically and mentally abused for the past 13 years, then in

CHAPTER FOUR

the space of one day I had been told it was time for me to go into society and contribute. Whatever that meant. I just wanted to return to my home, so I tried to work in the city, I went through numerous jobs, always getting fired for being lazy or for drinking. I didn't drink but those accusations made me want to try it. So I did, with the little money I made I went to a liquor store and bought a bottle of whiskey. It burned as I drank it straight from the bottle. My head dizzy, my feet stumbled, and I kept on drinking. The next day my head hurt, my mouth felt like it was stuffed with cotton balls. I was thirsty. I had no money for food but I knew a restaurant that threw out food that hadn't been sold from the night before. I wondered why they threw it out, it was like a feast compared to what I had grown up with in the residential school. I found whole sandwiches and ate. As I sat in the park I realized I hadn't had a bad thought the night before, I couldn't remember what I had thought but I knew I didn't think of the school I had left not long ago. The memories of the hands that slapped or pinched, the glaring eyes, the basement room. I sat under the trees on the grass, smelling the air and thinking of what I could do in the city, I had no skills, I looked different than the other workers here, all I knew was pain and torture. I fell asleep

CHAPTER FOUR

with a full belly, my headache fading away. I heard kids voices and immediately shut the murmurs down. No allowing the voices to enter my thoughts or I would never get into heaven. Soon I was snoring lightly. I awoke to someone kicking my booted foot. An officer of the law glaring harshly at me and telling me bums were not allowed to sleep in the park. I tried to tell him I wasn't a bum but my voice only mumbled incoherently and I immediately rose and listened to his directions. Never thinking to ask where I could go. I had only one set of clothes and it had been awhile since I bathed, the sisters, though mean, always made sure my clothes were clean and kept us bathed.

I saw a man sitting at the edge of the park. There was a blue tarp and some cardboard boxes piled up behind him. He had a long scruffy beard which blended into his long curly hair. Like me he had on blue jeans and boots and a long sleeve button up top. But he looked cleaner his eyes brown and clear. He had a book in his hands, I had always like reading. The stories in the bible had intrigued me, and it made the Sisters happy when I knew an answer to one of the questions they asked. I approached the man and asked what he was reading. He turned from his book and

CHAPTER FOUR

looked up at me. With a wide smile he said it was a book on Philosophy. I laughed and asked if he was learning anything. And he replied that he learned something every single day. But it didn't always come from a book. He invited me to sit and talk with him and so I did. His name was Henry and he was my first friend outside of the residential school. He talked about his Philosophy book and how he wanted to change the world. As the hours went on we learned about one another, he was divorced, no kids and he had been addicted to drugs, when his wife found out about how much he was spending on the illegal stuff she cleaned out their bank account and left him then divorced him shortly after. Instead of making him stop, it made him depressed and the only way he found to cope was to do more drugs. He soon lost his job and then his house, all his friends seemed to disappear just as quickly as his wife had. After a year he had lost everything and he was living on the streets. Hours later he looked up at the sky and told me it was supper time at the soup kitchen and we had better hurry or we would miss out. I had no idea what a soup kitchen was but I knew I was hungry and my hands were starting to shake. We walked with purpose towards a red brick building I stumbled a step as I realized we were going into a church. I hadn't been away from the

CHAPTER FOUR

residential school system for long and a rush of emotion came from me, Henry stopped and looked back at me his eyes questioning my pause. My legs went rubbery and I sat heavily on the stone steps. Taking a step down Henry quietly asked me if I was ok. Swallowing the bile that rose up my throat I quickly shook my head in the negative. Henry was the first person I had shared my experiences with at the residential school and I was grateful he was here with me now. I noticed other people slowly entering the building a couple of them nodding to each other in greeting. Sitting down beside me, Henry explained to me in quiet tones that the soup kitchen was downstairs in the hall and it was run by volunteers, there would be a hot soup or some chilli and a ham sandwich or maybe tuna if we were lucky today. There was always a piece of fruit that we could carry out to eat later on so we wouldn't go hungry overnight. Even quieter he whispered that there were no priests or nuns around and he would stay with me while inside. We entered the hall and from there I found a new family, people who shared their stories, alcohol, cardboard boxes and tarps. I forgot about heading home to the reservation.

CHAPTER FIVE

Feet planted firmly in the present, I look around the dilapidated building. Wondering for the umpteenth time if the haunting memories would ever disappear, for myself and the many other children who had suffered here. All the help I had along my path with my shelter friends, many who have passed on now due to harsh living conditions combined with their various addictions, Elder John who will forever walk beside me until I travel my final journey and my own family who I have been connecting with over the last few years. I feel the urgent need to help others, not only with my visions, the feeling is nagging at me. I must get my emotions under control, no over emotional outbursts. It had been my key to survival so far. I briefly remember the feeling of emotion the first time I actively let the voices in my head converse with me years after leaving the residential school. I remember being so terrified.

I thought I was going a bit crazy, after all who hears voices in their head when no one is around. I listened to the voice first then harshly remembered the nuns telling me I was never going to get into Heaven if I kept listening to the voices and abruptly slammed the door closed. Terrified and shaking I went to the water and listened to the waves roll

CHAPTER FIVE

across the rocks, the wind whistling softly through the trees I sat and ran my hands along the green, sweet smelling grass. I found my centre and gently eased the door open to the voices I had heard. It was hard work, I had to distinguish each person or my mind would be a scrambled mess. Ever fearful that I wouldn't get into Heaven I had to slowly let the voices in. Gradually, I learned that each person or voice had a distinct hue and if I could concentrate on the colour I could hear only that person talking. I was wet with sweat the first time I let a voice through, terrified of being struck down by God. After awhile I learned to block out the voices when I was within earshot of other living people. They tended to get freaked out by a native guy wandering around the park talking to himself. I had had the cops called on me to many times to remember. While most of the boys in blue had been nice there were also a few bad apples who just pushed or yelled at me to move on and quit bothering the nice people who were playing or walking in the park.

Shaking my head, I got into the present again, I knew the memories were what I needed to find the closure or the forgiveness needed to move

CHAPTER FIVE

on in my life but I was feeling over run with strong emotions and I felt like my visions were

going to be a step backwards. With a look around the kitchen I turned and headed toward the front of the building, wondering if I would see Roseanne again before I left.

Leaving the building the stone steps crumbled a bit under my shoes, I headed to my truck to leave but then had the urge to turn around and start walking around the building. The ground was uneven, dirt and grass vying for space to grow. The dirt was winning.

At the rear of the building I saw an old skating ring and two wooden benches on either side. The rink had long been overgrown with weeds, the paint peeled off the benches. There were four outbuildings here, we were never allowed to look in these buildings. The roofs had caved in on all of them, tall weeds had grown up and through the window holes. My curiosity got the better of me and I made my way to the closest building. The door had been pulled off the hinges and now leaned up against the wooden structure. Gingerly, I stepped inside the building, careful of the

CHAPTER FIVE

roof and all the wooden splinters around the door frame. My eyes adjusted to the darkness and I saw a couple of old shovels and rakes lying on the ground. Shuddering at the implication of the tools I looked around at the rest of the contents. A couple paint cans, some gardening tools and a rusty ladder. I turned to exit the building and thought I should go to the hill and go to the bottom to pay my respects to the children who had been buried there years before. Even after all these years the bodies of countless unidentified children's bodies lay beneath the uneven grass. Buried without so much as a prayer, the older boys shovelling dirt over their friends, wrapped only in canvas tarp, bound together with yellow rope. The families who had long ago said hurried goodbyes to their children when the Government Officials came to their land with vans to load up with any child they could get their hands on between the ages of 4 and 16. They thought the younger, the better, to assimilate or be adopted into a "white" household. The last pictures many Aboriginal families had were of their child or children being torn from their arms, tears streaming, crying to stay with their family. Many adopted out and never finding home again, so many young ones never knowing the happiness I had known surrounded by the elders of the community.

CHAPTER FIVE

Shame washed over me as I thought how I had wasted years being angry, taking my anger out on my friends, I knew I had to go home, reconnect to nature, my family, my heritage before I could be whole again.

Standing on the mound of uneven grass, looking up at the sky, the fluffy white clouds moving lazily by, I hear laughter. I quickly look around to see who might be here in the field, I see a group of children playing tag, their peals of laughter make me smile. I close my eyes and take in their happiness. Glad that there can be happy memories made here. I immediately sense a difference in the still air and hold my breath expectantly.

"Hello Mark" I hear a familiar singsong voice say

"Mary?" I ask in a choked voice

Little Mary who helped me in school, her shy smile, her kind eyes. We were friends until she left without saying goodbye to me. She was younger than me but years older in experience.

CHAPTER FIVE

"Yes Mark, I'm here. I have missed you for so many years. I wanted to tell you that I am ok. I take care of the others left here. We will be ok but we would like to go home and be with our families. I know you are busy and your journey is not to be with us right now but I persisted and was allowed this one conversation with you. Our Creator is humble and pleased you are finally finding your way home." Mary quietly informed me

Keeping my eyes closed I treasure her singsong voice, oh how I had missed her laugh. A million questions rush to be asked but I only ask one,

"Is there anything I can do for you, before I leave?" I ask her

"Just knowing you are on your way makes me happy, safe travels" she answers. She quietly continues saying, "However, I would like for you to take this advice with you on your journey Mark. We all made friends in this school, some of us didn't make it home and never will we have the chance to, but we are hopeful that in the years to come, you and other

CHAPTER FIVE

survivors will find your peace. We mostly have, we also have each other. We are not to leave these grounds unless we are taken home by our families and at this time some of our families don't even know we are here. So please, when you have finished your journey, come back and help us unite with our loved ones."

A tear fell from my eye for Mary, her family and all the unclaimed children buried around the country. My heart in pieces I promise to come back and take her home. Hoping I will be able to heal some of the broken families and bring closure to many of the missing children. Finally, hopefully the families would be able to grieve, mourn their children and start the long road to healing. I need to help them all, that is why I am here but I need to forgive before I can help.

"Thank you Mark, now I believe you have someplace to go. Be well. Safe travels again my friend. Creator watch over you as your journey begins." Her tinkling voice drifts further away.

"Bye Mary, be safe" I said as she fades away.

CHAPTER FIVE

Opening my eyes I wipe the tears away. Saying a prayer to Creator for my friends and the many others buried here. I turn and walk slowly towards my car. Behind me I hear Mary laugh, the wonderful sunny laugh that had helped me through many sad nights when I missed my family, the others greet her warmly and they continue on with their game of tag. My steps falter, is this part of my journey, I wonder. Then remembering Mary say it wasn't our time, I continue on.

Realizing that I hadn't had dinner I climb into my truck and decide I need to eat and make a plan. What was I going to do, how was I going to find peace and move on, was it possible to do just because I had a time limit? These questions raced through my mind and I tried to slow them down, one step at a time is all I could do. Driving down the rutted drive I look in my rear view mirror, standing on the steps are Mary and the children waving goodbye. I would come back and help them I promise myself. I raise my hand in farewell as they disappear.

CHAPTER FIVE

*Sina
you are the best
sister in the world.
I Love You ♡*

CHAPTER SIX

I stop in at a truck stop roadside diner. It looks like a busy place. I realize I haven't had a drink or bite to nibble on since I had left Detective Viv hours earlier. I hope I can grab a quick good bite to eat and keep on going. Now that I have a destination in mind I am anxious to get there. I have been reconnecting with some members of my family lately but I hadn't wanted to leave the city, I have been keeping a large part of myself away from them. The occasional obligatory phone call at Christmas, which had me thinking. Why were we celebrating the birth of Christ? In my thinking I had nothing to celebrate this birthday for. This person if he even ever existed had brought nothing but heartache for my Aboriginal people. Maybe it hadn't started out as an extinction but it had certainly ended with this thinking. The good Christians trying to assimilate the natives to the mainstream way of life. They certainly hadn't asked us if we wanted to celebrate Christs birth. Nowadays it's mostly a commercial holiday anyways. Stores vying for the ability to have your hard earned money spent on frivolous items for children around the globe. Commercialism, bah humbug. Even as I thought the word I laughed, the word was even commercialized brought to light by a children's Christmas movie. Small changes are all I could think as I pushed open the finger smudged glass door to the diner. If I could help myself then I could help others.

CHAPTER SIX

The waitress walked by with a coffee pot in her hand, smiling at me she said "find yourself a seat, I will be right there with a menu" she kept walking towards a table with a lone truck driver seated there and filled his coffee cup up. I wandered over to a window booth and slid in. The red vinyl seats were ripped in spots and had been taped together hoping for a bit more life from them. The waitress came by and asked if I wanted a coffee as she placed a menu down in front of me.

"A diet soda please" I reply with a smile.

"Sure thing honey" she answers "lunch special today is a single clubhouse with fries or soup, soup is minestrone, I will just go get your diet soda and be right back" turning away with a smile she goes to get my drink. I wonder how many times a day she has to do that spiel.

I glance briefly at the menu and decide to go with the special, its probably quick. The waitress returns with my drink and I ask her for the special on brown bread with the minestrone soup. I look around at the

CHAPTER SIX

diner, people from all walks of life are here. They look tired though. Long hours away from their homes and families. I try to take a quiet moment to sort my thoughts and prepare for the journey ahead. Going over my conversations the last few hours. Remembering my grandmother Roseanne, how young she looked when I first encountered her. Realizing that I hadn't before had a vision age like that I closed my eyes to remember her. Wondering if I would see her again and hoping I would.

My Nohkom, Roseanne, was the first person to notice my visions. I was about 3 years old and had been telling her of my night dreams, the warriors who I saw and told her when they seemed to speak directly to me. The language was not the same as ours but I seemed to understand every word. She listened intently to me nodding her head and encouraging me to try to converse with them in any way I could.

I remember telling her that the warrior in my dream was watching tv in our living room so I could talk to her. She was startled but asked me what he wanted. I told her he missed the warm fire and the conversation with his brothers. My grandmother was quiet a moment and asked if I could tell the

CHAPTER SIX

warrior to go to the centre of the village where the big teepee stood. Immediately I said ok, he's heading that way. She gathered me up and we went to a few houses on our way to the teepee and as we arrived there the fire was burning warmly as it always was. We were the first to arrive but quickly a few men joined us and they began to beat their drums and started singing a melancholy song about survival, about coming home and then changing the beat to a more upbeat sound they smiled as they sang of brotherhood and family and women gathering to care for everyone in the village. I smiled and clapped my hands as more warriors joined the one who had been watching tv in my living room only minutes before. He smiled and greeted his brothers with warm hugs all of them singing along with the drummers surrounding the fire. He glanced at me and smiled happily, singing as he and his brothers disappeared from my view. I said good bye and my grandmother wrapped me in a hug with tears in her eyes she thanked the drummers for their song and said the warriors were happily reunited and heading home with all our help. A few of the drummers went home and a few stayed happily drumming a quiet song. I noticed some of the elders of

CHAPTER SIX

my community come sit by the fire wrapped in blankets to ward off the chill. I hoped they would tell a story it was one of my favourite things. My Kokum gestured to me to come closer to her, not my real Kokum but everyone in the village called her that and she loved us all, like we were her very own children. Roseanne was my real Nohkom. I happily climbed up onto my Kokums lap eager to hear her story.

With a low voice Kokum started her story about our warrior ancestors, how they roamed the lands protecting the chief and all the princesses in the tribe. They hunted and brought fresh bison to the people each sharing the gift they had. The women would fish and gather berries and all would gather around the fire to tell stories of Turtle Island. The people lived in harmony with others and with the animals who shared the land. But the greed would come, the Earth would be ravaged of its resources. The story goes that the Warriors of the Rainbow would be there to help guide and restore the Earth to all its glory where the people lived in harmony their hearts pure and warm with all mankind.

CHAPTER SIX

I was startled out of my daydream when the waitress put a plate down in front of me with my sandwich and soup on it.

Looking up at her I said, "Thank you" my voice quiet.

"Your welcome" she answered, "would you like a water or another diet soda?"

"A water would be great, thank you" I answer her with a smile

I watch as she walks away to get me a water. I have a bite into my sandwich, mmm it is pretty good. Soon my fingers are sticky with melted butter and toast crumbs running down them and landing back onto my plate. I guess I should make time to eat properly throughout the day. The soup is hot and tasty and I hurry to finish my meal and get back on the road. Drinking the icy cold water that the waitress placed on my table, I rinse my mouth and cool it down after the hot soup. My belly full, I am ready to pay the bill and head out, eager to to my destination.

CHAPTER SEVEN

The drive to the reservation is a couple hours from here. I am unsure what to expect when I return. Where would I stay, no one knew I was returning today. I hadn't called anyone to tell them to expect me. I suppose I had some family members who would put up with me for a day or two.

Letting my mind wander I turn my radio up and sing loudly along with a song I know. The beat vibrating the windows as I speed along the lonely road. Before I know it, I am passing the welcome sign inviting all to enter the land bordering my reservation. Turning the music down I slow to within the posted speed limit.

My first stop would be to the convenience store. I need gas, a drink and I could use a bathroom stop too. The store is a trailer sitting on concrete pilings, there's a rickety wooden wheelchair ramp and fireworks advertised for sale in the smudged front windows.

CHAPTER SEVEN

Feeling more nervous than I should, I pay for my stuff and head over to my Nohkom, Roseanne's, old house. Not sure who I will find living there now. Nothing really seems to have changed here, the roads are still gravel, the big teepee still stands in the centre of the village although there are wooden benches around the outside of it now where before we had just used logs to sit on. People, old and young still walk along the gravel road stopping to converse with one another, smiling and laughing. The pace is slower here than in the city, there seems to be less urgency. The little brown house still stands on the small hill just down the road. The creek seems smaller that I remember, the trees seem less dense, the forest I had played in as a child seems smaller. When I returned here the first time I was shocked at the overgrown grass, the unpainted wooden dwellings. They all seemed dimmer than my childhood memories, where everything was awash in sunlight, the grass was green and soft under our bare feet. The trees towered over us as we ran and played endless games in them. Finding berries growing in abundance by the creek beds which always seemed full of fish. Even the wild animals which stopped by the creek to grab a drink and eat some grass seemed majestic to me. I guess I had to grow up and see things how they really were, I now looked at all

CHAPTER SEVEN

those things with "white" eyes. Parking the car I went to the front door and before I could knock the screen door was flung open and a girl with long unbound hair came flying out and hurdled into my arms in a full two arm hug.

"Oh your finally home!" She said "I cant wait to tell everyone, we will have a feast to celebrate"

She abruptly let me go and turned to yell into the house "he's here guys!" Grabbing me by the arm she turned to look at me and I was startled by her beautiful smile, her eyes seemed to twinkle with delight. Racking my brain I tried to put her face to a name I had long since forgotten.

"Maryrose?" I asked

"Of course its me big brother!" She replied, her smile faltering a little bit she asked "don't you remember me"

CHAPTER SEVEN

My eyes teared up as I remembered the little baby my mother had kept on her back as my cousins and I were taken by the government people so many years ago. Her dark curly hair and smile the same. How had I forgotten about her, I chastised myself and all my faults for missing out on seeing her again. I had wasted my life on regret and hatred and had forgot about my family.

My head hanging down I said, "of course its you, all grown up now. I'm sorry I missed it."

She smiled her radiant smile again and said "but you're here now!"

I was immediately surrounded by people hugging me and welcoming me home, I didn't need to stop for a drink as I was offered food and drink by no less than five people who took their turn hugging me. I was feeling completely overwhelmed I didn't know these people, I had run away from them and they were all so happy to see me again. After I had hugged the final person I was pulled into the house and onto a couch with brown, yellow and orange flowers on it, it had definitely seen better days. The

CHAPTER SEVEN

wooden frame was peeling in places the cushions flattened by all the bottoms that had sat down there over the years. The linoleum flooring was yellowed with age and corners of it were peeling away from the sub floor. The tv sat in the corner on a tv stand made of pressboard. Which didn't look very sturdy. There were dozens of different sized pictures hanging in different sized and colour frames on the wall. My family I thought quickly, I didn't really recognize any of the people except my grandmother. I got to my feet, still hearing the excited voices talking over each other at my arrival and went to look at a photo. Nohkom was young, just like I had seen her in the residential school kitchen. She was wearing a long blue dress, I wonder if I had subconsciously saw this picture beforehand and she had appeared to me how I remembered her. In this photo, she had a lot of people standing beside her. I remember seeing a couple of them around the campfire that had sent the warriors home from that long ago dream/vision. My vision blurred but I stopped the feeling. No visions right now. I needed a clear head. I needed to talk with these people, my family. My family. I thought with a smile.

CHAPTER SEVEN

Happy with myself I remembered my grandmother's warm hug, I turned back to everyone who had assembled in the room to see me. A few of them were looking at me with weary eyes and a few with expectancy in theirs. What were they wanting from me, what kind of speech were they expecting. I took a deep breath and looked into a few brown eyes and began.

"Thank you for welcoming me so warmly, Nohkom misses you all but is happy on her journey now." A few of them looked at each other with questions in their eyes. My little sister, Maryrose, clapped her hands and smiled wide again. I smiled back at her.

"Nohkom told me to return home and that I had to continue my journey here so here I am." I told everyone. There was only a second of a pause, even the air seemed to stand still.

Then all at once a few of the older men started asking question,
"When did you see her"
"Is she happy"

CHAPTER SEVEN

"Did she see the new grand babies born"

"Is uncle Robert with her"

They were overlapping each other yelling out questions and I laughed at their exuberance. I could sense the change in the air, the acceptance. I was home. I was a part of the fabric of this community, even after years of neglecting them, they accepted me with no boundaries. It was like I had never left them. This is family I thought. They will accept me here, as I am, troubled, tormented and terrified but they will accept me.

"You don't seem confused that I had a conversation with her?" I asked the room at large.

"You probably don't remember me, but my name is Junior" said a stout looking man. His long dark hair pulled back in a tight braid, his eyes danced with laughter and mischief. He immediately reminded me of Elder John.

CHAPTER SEVEN

I smiled at him as I replied "I do, I am sure we caught fish together in the stream when we were young boys"

"Yup that's me" he replied with a grin, "anyways, I remember you talking with the elders when we were younger and how they told you that it was a blessing to have the gift of communication with the people who have left this plane and headed on to their final journey, so of course, you are kind of a legend around here. We would all like to know how our loved ones are and if their passing was smooth…but what I really want to know is, what does Creator look like? Is he a he or she?" He leaned forward in his chair eager to hear my answer. His sparkling eyes looked expectantly in mine waiting to hear my answer.

I smiled and wondered how I could have forgotten how everyone just fits, this mishmash of family members were so different yet they fit together like one. The community that had been ripped apart was still standing after so many years of abuse and neglect. My heart felt a little lighter as I looked around.

CHAPTER SEVEN

Laughing a little "I don't know if Creator is a he or she" I answered Junior "I assume Creator is whatever you need them to be at the moment your looking for answers"

Looking a little let down Junior sits back in his chair only to bounce back up again because there was a little squeal behind him. One of the little girls had snuck onto his chair while he was leaning forward. The group roared with laughter at his shocked look and then they looked back to my sister again when she directed a few people to do chores for the feast that would be happening tonight. A feast for me, a celebration for my arrival back to the community. I had a feeling my little sister had taken on the matriarchal position in the family, I was proud of her for keeping everyone together and I looked forward to talking with her more later on. In the back of my mind I wondered if she had been taken to residential school too, and if so, how had she come to be so happy and whole. Had she been beaten, ridiculed, taunted, pinched, spit upon, had she been sexually violated. My heart beat faster, my fist clenched in rage. Feel the anger, breath through it, let it go. My mantra that had gotten me through life.

CHAPTER SEVEN

The questions stayed with me all through the long night, there was a feast, enough food to feed the whole village it seemed. I think most of the village turned out to see me and welcome me back, young people and old people and every age in between seemed to know who I was. There was a fire in a huge brick fire pit in the backyard. Dozens of chairs, white lawn chairs, some kitchen chairs even a rocker recliner were strewn about with one or two people sitting on each one. Someone had brought out music and speakers however it was so noisy that I'm not sure the music was even on. The food was mouth watering a mixture of traditional food and popular junk food. I had a bit of everything until I was over full. There was a clothes line with some jeans hung up to dry, I guess my arrival had put a stop to laundry day. There were people coming and going to the backyard, pausing to chat or give a hug or an arm punch to each other. In time every person there stopped to talk to me. It seemed everyone wanted to know if I had contacted a certain person that they missed or just wanted to know how I did it, the talking to spirits. I kind of grew tired of their question, this was not why I had come here. I needed to forgive my abusers. That was my journey. How could that happen

CHAPTER SEVEN

among these carefree people. It seemed there were no hidden agendas in this group, what you see is what you get I thought. There was one older man who everyone seemed to stop and ask if he needed anything, tea, bannock and dry meat always seem to be within his reach. He had kind eyes, thanking everyone who stopped to talk to him, he spoke quietly and listened intently to all. Everyone who left him seemed happier like he gave them hope or they had heard exactly what they needed to hear from him. I felt the need to speak to him push me across the room, and before I knew what I wanted to say to him I was standing directly in front of him. I knelt down so we could be eye to eye.

"Hello" I said "my name is Mark Whitestone, I think I remember you from when I was a child. And I believe you are in the picture with my Nohkom hanging on the wall."

"I am" his ancient gravelly voice answered me.
"My name is Albert, I am your grandmothers brother."

CHAPTER SEVEN

"I don't know if you would remember this but were you there singing with your drum the night we sent the warriors home?" I asked

"I was" he answered me as he took a sip of his tea.

He didn't offer anything else and I was unsure how to ask him about the residential school and why the kids were taken from this village. I knew he was the reason I returned here, well the one main reason. After being here for a few hours, sober and listening to the laughter, stories, the community who still rallied behind me. I felt more at home here than anywhere else I had been since I was 5 years old. It was time to come home as my Nohkom had told me.

"May I call you Nimosom" I questioned Albert

"I would be honoured if you called me that, young man" Albert replied

CHAPTER SEVEN

"I see the people who look after you here, you are very loved by everyone" I said to Nimosom

"They are young and know I am old, and not long for this world. They are good children" he replied "Like you, they come to me with many questions and I help in any way I can"

I listened to the timber of his voice, it was strong in his frail body, he was my Nohkom's brother so he must be advanced in his age. I gathered my thoughts and tried to be diplomatic in wording my question.

"Would it be ok to ask you about the Government People who came and took the children away from the reservation all those years ago?" I hastily spit out, so much for diplomacy.

Immediately, it seemed the music got quieter, the voices quieted, and a few people came and sat on the floor in front of Nimosom many eyes looked toward him and he straightened out in his chair, took another sip of tea and answered me.

CHAPTER SEVEN

"It was a long time ago, for many generations the Government People had come to our village in the fall and attempted to take as many children as could fit into their vans. Sometimes it was only one or two little ones and sometimes it was many more. I can still hear their cries and the cries of all their families. It echoes in my mind everyday. Your story, Mark, involves many children. Although everyone is important we were hurt to see you taken. We had waited years for a child who had the vision, your abilities were prophesied many, many years before you were born. When you arrived your were blind for three days. In that time you were visited by others on the other plane and they prepared you for your life with us. After those three days you were healed, you saw and heard everything and soaked up knowledge like you had been born to do. The Elders cared for you and sang for you. They taught you the traditional ways and our legends to be passed on to the next generations. We didn't know you were going to be taken from us so soon. We hid you the first year in hopes the priest and nuns wouldn't come again but every year after the fall harvest they showed up. For many years we hid children in the bush down by the water but we could never be sure when they would show up, sometimes

CHAPTER SEVEN

it was in the middle of the night when we were asleep and they would take the children right from their beds." He sighed and shook his head. His eyes watering he looked at me and nodded. Like he had just made up his mind about something important.

By this time everyone who had been visiting and laughing had found a spot to sit and listen to Nimosom speak. The quiet man held the attention of everyone and all he had to do was speak quietly. The importance of this man was staggering. My heart beat faster as I leaned in to listen to his story. I had been waiting to hear this my whole life. I felt the warm arms of my Nohkom surround me, the smell of pine cones seemed to hover everywhere as I sat and listened to her brother. I looked around and no one else seemed to see, hear or smell her so I just let her hold me as I listened.

"Every year, the families left behind after the young ones were taken, were changed. Bitterness filled them day after day. The children were taken, but, there were some adults who tried to get them back. They were unsuccessful though, we never were told where the children went, where

CHAPTER SEVEN

you went." He spoke this to me. "We were told the children would get a good education so they could learn to live with the white people off the reserve. It would be better for them than staying here and living in tents, as that is what the white people called our teepees."

Nimosom looked around at those gathered in front of him and patted some of their heads, touched their hair.

"Sometimes the kids came home to us in the summer, they were changed though, no longer spoke our language. Our Creator seemed to have been beaten out of them and replaced with their christian God. The families would try to find their way back to the days before the children left and some made it close, only to have the government people come again in the fall and take them back again. The children would scream and cry but there was no use fighting, they always won. It was a type of genocide, they were trying to change our ways. They were sent *to beat the Indian out of the child*. They very nearly succeeded. It has been a long time trying to forgive, many have not and their hearts are blackened with grief and hatred." Nimosom glanced at me before he continued his story. "It is our way to try forgiveness, to live the best we can and continue or

CHAPTER SEVEN

traditions. Our numbers are small as there have been many lost to this life, it has been Creator who has led us to our path right now, it is up to each of you to make the decision who to follow. You are our future, it is the young ones who will look to you for guidance. They follow your path whether it is a good path or a deceitful path. It is up to each of you, our next generation, to contribute to the well being of our culture, treasure it, pass it on, share with all who would listen. Forgiveness is not what you give to others in response to a mistake they made, forgiveness is what you give yourself for going on your individual path. Forgive yourselves, your heart will be lighter and will enable you to see your next path clearer." He paused to take another sip of tea.

"We are still finding forgiveness for the children who have not returned, we ask Creator to care for them and guide them when needed. The ones who are able to return home and find their forgiveness, we pray for their return. One day we will all be together again and until that day, we have this little piece of home for all our relations to gather." He stopped and looked at me.

CHAPTER SEVEN

"We are happy you are home Mark and you are welcome anytime to stay. The fish are plentiful and your home awaits your return. I hope you will find your forgiveness and take your place in the community, which has always adored you and prayed for your safe return as we have prayed for all the children." He waited a moment before he rose from his seat, immediately the boy closest to him jumped up to help him stand. Nimosom looked at me, or not quite at me, and smiled and winked at something or someone just over my right shoulder. I felt my Nohkom release me from her hug and whisper away.

"I am tired," Nimosom said, "Mark, would you walk an old man home now"

I found my sisters eyes and she shook her head yes.

"Of course, Nimosom" I answered

A young girl about ten years old said she would walk with us so we wouldn't get lost.

CHAPTER SEVEN

As we were leaving everyone there seemed to shake Nimosom's hand or kiss his weathered cheek, thanking him for his story. The three of us set off on the gravel driveway, I thought we would drive but he said walking is better for the soul. We walked slowly in compatible silence the little girl singing a sweet song for us. The air was fresh and woodsy, not like anything you could smell in the big city. As I walked in my runners I thought of the springy grass that had skimmed across my bare feet when I was young. I noticed a couple of dogs come to trot beside us. Nothing fancy or pampered about these little guys. Their fur was matted with mud, probably because they swam in the river. It was hard to know if they were brown or black haired. They looked healthy enough though. They were probably hoping for a bit of leftovers from the feast we had just left. The little girl giggled and petted them as they bumped their heads against her legs.

"It was nice to see her" Nimosom said, his deep voice breaking the dark silence. "My sister is just as beautiful as ever, thank you for bringing

CHAPTER SEVEN

her to me Mark. I will join her very soon, although I am not in any hurry as we just got you back here."

Startled I looked over at him, "you could see her" I almost yelled.

No one had said that to me before.

"No, I couldn't see her, but I knew she was with you. There was a beautiful blue glow over your shoulder and I swear I could smell pine cones . Blue was her favourite colour. She said it reminded her of the vastness of the sky and all its possibilities." He laughed, "my favourite colour is green in case you need to know that for future knowledge"

I laughed and said that I would tuck it away for when I might need it.

"I understand you have a journey to travel, I hope you know that any questions I can help you with, I will." He told me.

CHAPTER SEVEN

"I am having trouble with the forgiveness part or maybe I just want to know why. I am angry with the government for not seeing our people as human, could they not see it, our culture, our family units, our connection with the land and all it provided us with." My gut was churning as I went over the destruction in my mind. "We would have shared our knowledge, our bounty

with them, the Colonizers. How long did this trauma have to go on. They changed us and our belief system. Human nature was changed for us and our future generations. How will we ever recover, can our people ever return to our traditional ways. Can we survive this." My breathing was broken and ragged my steps faltered and stopped. I took Nimosom by the hand, his brown wrinkled skin I thought it would be fragile, delicate because of his age but I found his hands warm, weathered by life, strong and they gripped mine tightly. "Did our families, our community, know the torture we endured in those residential schools"

My voice broke as I tried to describe my horror to him. I told him everything. My voice howled with the injustice to our people, the children.

CHAPTER SEVEN

It was like I had no control, the words poured out of me from the bottom of my soul. My heart ached for Mother Earth, how could we begin to heal. I told Nimosom how I had been trying to heal the last few years. How hard it had been and still was. How come I was not healing, where could I find the forgiveness needed to move on with my life. I told him about Elder John, and my partnership with him. How I had finally began to put my life together only to lose him, I was like a ship afloat in the sea with no direction. I told him about the little kids who I needed to help get home and about Detective Viv and her tired eyes. I told him about the residential school trip I just had and the spirit of Mary who had visited me and asked for my help to get them home to their communities or to their families so they could leave the horror behind and move to their final resting place. I admitted I was overwhelmed and didn't know where to start. I told him about seeing my Nohkom and talking to her and the bottle of water that had come out of the fridge, cold and refreshing and then disappeared. The actual hug I had gotten from her. Seeing the little brown haired girl jump from the roof and telling me she was finally free. Then finally of leaving Mary and of the children waving at me in my rear view mirror. I gulped in air feeling like I would never get enough. I slowly

CHAPTER SEVEN

noticed that my cheeks were wet with tears and I hastily wiped them away. I still held onto his hands, gripping them tightly, afraid to let go.

Nimosom was quiet the whole time I was talking. He hadn't interrupted me but listened to all I had said. In his gravelly voice he asked me, "How do you feel after telling me your story Mark" he gently removed his hands and reversed his hold, now he was gently holding my large hands in his. I felt safe. A feeling I hadn't had in many many years.

I thought about how I felt, taking in my mood, how I was walking shoulders back, head held high since I had been here. I listened to my heart, it was beating evenly. Letting go of my hands, we continued walking in silence. I noticed the little girl had slipped her hand into mine. It felt right. I wasn't gripping her had to tightly. She happily skipped along beside me. The dogs trotting along behind us happily smelling clumps of grass and moving along if it wasn't the right bush or grassy area to do their business. This is life, right here, I thought. This is how life is suppose to be.

CHAPTER SEVEN

"I suppose I feel lighter" I said out loud to Nimosom.

"Maybe that is what you need to focus on, that feeling of lightness in your heart. No one should bear all their troubles in silence, that is what your family is there for." He patted my shoulder with his frail hand. "This is my house, thank you for the company Mark, I hope you will come back soon. Our community needs strong leaders like you to lead the young ones on a clean path. We can wait a little longer for your return."

He bent down to the little girl and told her to make sure I found my way home fast. She laughed and said, "goodbye uncle" and hugged his frail shoulders. He went inside his little house and we watched as a single lamp turned on then we turned to walk back to my sisters house.

The little girl looked up at me and said, "my mom said your special and we should welcome you home. Why are you special."

I looked down at her and said "I'm not to sure why I am special but my Nohkom told me I was and so I believed her."

CHAPTER SEVEN

"Well, you look pretty normal to me" she said

Smiling at her blunt straightforward way of talking I said "thank you, I always wanted to be just normal"

As we walked in silence, the reservation dogs happily trotting beside us, I appreciated the time to think about the story Nimosom had told and the way he had told me I needed to think of myself as lighter. I really felt like my worries had left, I was lighter, maybe this was what I needed. To know I belonged somewhere. I had always belonged here. The people, my people, needed me, he had said. I knew I could help here, I knew in my heart they needed me here. I smiled as I walked along. Thinking how easy it was going to be to leave the city and my apartment. I was needed here and that's all I knew for sure.

Before long we were back at my sisters, the partygoers had all but left, a few stragglers had stayed to help clean up the yard and the dishes that were piled around the kitchen. I pitched in to help fold chairs and put

CHAPTER SEVEN

them back in the shed at the back of the house, the long white tables were washed and folded and put away until next time they were needed. Before long the house had returned to its former shabby self. Although I didn't look at it that way now, I saw the happy faces, the easy going conversations, the way this house belonged to a family, my family, and they wanted me here. I finally fit somewhere.

Alone in the living room I went to my Nohkom pictured on the wall, she smiled back at me, "Thank you Nohkom for sending me here" I whispered to her.

"Welcome home my boy" her voice whispered in my ear and I felt her hug me one last time.

Yes, I thought to myself, I am home.

CHAPTER EIGHT

The next 24 hours were a mixture of laughter and tears. I was welcomed into this collection of misfits, each one bringing something special to the group. We talked long into the night until even the animals had went to sleep. I was given a lumpy bed to sleep on with some patched up blankets, it was the best dreamless sleep I had had in years. I visited with Nimosom the next day bringing with me some fresh caught fish we had cleaned and scaled earlier in the day. He told some of the stories I hadn't heard for many years. He also said he was lonely in his house all by himself and that when I came around I could stay with him. There would be a room made up for me and waiting. I thanked him for sharing his stories and assured him that I would be back as soon as I could. I had a lot to finish up in the city and with my job, but I would be back.

I found out the little girl was my sisters daughter, her name was Markie, named after me. I was touched. I had spent the most time talking with my sister, Maryrose, we even went for a walk around her yard, holding hands, it was like she needed to make sure I was really there. She

CHAPTER EIGHT

told me she had been taken to the residential school but it wasn't the same as the one I went to. While the nuns had been mean she hadn't been abused like I had, she cried silent tears as I had replayed my years in the school system. She was happy when I told her of Elder John and his role in keeping me sober and finding a job I was able to do. I told her of how I had started opening the door to the voices and the many people who had tried to connect with me. Although I was hesitant to tell her why I had stopped I think she guessed the reason. She encouraged me to keep connecting with the many people who needed my help and she was amazed to think that I could still talk with people who had passed on to the next part of their journey. She told me she remembered stories our mother told of me when she was little. I had been gone, but for six years she got to stay with our family they told stories of the children who had left the reserve. She said the elders prayed in the big teepee for the children who had been taken and that they would find their way home when Creator sent them. We talked about the many children who had not found their way home and the ones who had. They were hurt, scarred from their experiences, they were angry. She told me she didn't let alcohol on the reservation but the younger people always seemed to have some

CHAPTER EIGHT

inventive way of getting it in. She told me of their stories, there were a few who had gotten put into the social services system and some that were adopted into white families, she hoped they were fine, being looked after by the people who wanted them. My sister told me of the many kids who were still being taken off the reserve but now they were being taken by Children Social Services and there seemed to be nothing she could do to keep them unless she wanted to adopt them all. We finally got to the topic of Markie's father. He was a boy she had met in the residential school. They stayed friends all through school hiding their close friendship and as they were in their last year they made plans to stay together forever. They left the school together and found jobs in the small town nearby, and she got pregnant right away. They wanted to go home to their families but he didn't know exactly where he came from so they moved to her home and learned to love and live with her family and the elders welcomed him like one of their own sons. Things were good for a couple years but he was sad and missed his family even though he didn't know who they were. He began drinking and eventually he was so depressed he wandered off into the forest one night and he didn't return. She and Markie had been alone ever since. I said I was sorry I hadn't been

CHAPTER EIGHT

around to help her and Markie out. She just squeezed my hand and said she had been helped by the community and that Markie was a well rounded and inquisitive child.

As we talked I made another promise to myself, I would be a part of her family and help out her and Markie however they needed. I would never disappear on her again.

I found out everything I could about my sister and how she had taken over the band office. She had set up with the Elders a chief and counsel years ago and now they voted in new people every two years. She sat on many boards around the community and everyone seemed to ask her this or that when they needed any kind of help. She was kind, and had a beautiful soul. I envied her a little for the easy way she had with all the members of the reserve. She knew everyone's name, their kids names and even their Kokums and Mushoms. The community was at ease in her presence and I noticed her phone rang no less than a dozen times an hour. Little Markie was constantly helping her too. She answered the phone when her mom was busy with something else. I noticed the elders and

CHAPTER EIGHT

community members treat her with much respect especially for a child. Maryrose had a calming effect on others and I think people gravitated toward her to get that feeling. I noticed I had felt it, the easiness she had felt talking to me and listening to my story. I had recounted to her the tragedies I felt had been heaped on me and I hadn't felt the biting anger and despair I usually felt. Opening my wounds to her had been a balm to my soul, I admitted I felt lighter and actually looked forward to the future that was taking place in my mind with her and Markie and the community as a whole. I wondered about this feeling, was it happiness. It had been so many years since I had any notion of happiness I took a moment to enjoy the feeling. I smiled at my sister and squeezed her hand, she looked up at me and squeezed my hand back.

To soon it was time for me to leave as I had to return to my job in the city. I needed to help the kids who needed their final goodbyes with their families. I made plans with my sister to keep in touch, she knew I was planning on moving to the reserve soon and encouraged me to finish what I had to do in the city. I hugged her, Markie and everyone else who was there to see me off and promised to return as soon as I could.

CHAPTER EIGHT

With a glance over my shoulder I climbed into my truck and waved. Taking a mental picture of everyone gathered on the front steps to see me off. Markie holding on to her mother's hand smiling and yelling goodbye was my last picture of her. The whole group surrounded with what looked like clouds of blue. Holding them all in like a very large group hug.

CHAPTER NINE

Six months later

Sitting in my make shift office at the precinct, I twirled a plastic pen in my fingers as I read files and took notes. This part of my job had mostly been left to Elder John but since he had passed on I had had to take on the position. It was part of our contract with the police. I should look into hiring a person to help me out but who could possible fill the shoes left by John. I started to feel melancholy and gazed at a picture of him that sat beside my computer. I missed his quiet conversation. I picked up my phone to call my sister Maryrose and then put it back on the desk quietly removing my hand. I hadn't been able to call her since I had left the reservation six months ago. When I had returned home from my weekend visit I guess I got caught up in the work load and put all my energy into looking for the missing children, trying to find them and return them home. Then there was Detective Reynolds, she intrigued me. We had gotten closer since we had been on this case. Although, she is still quietly reserved and

CHAPTER NINE

shared little of her personal life, I had been putting together bits and pieces. Heaving a huge sigh, I admit I have just been avoiding calling my little sister. I'm not sure why. There was no pressure from her or anyone from the reserve to return home or numerous phone calls hassling me.

It kind of felt like they could live their lives with or without me. Was I really needed there or was my calling here in the city, helping out the police force. I knew I needed to make a choice. I thought of my apartment, bare, no family pictures on those walls. There had been no feasts to welcome me home, no little nieces holding my hand while on a walk. The grass in the city park seemed rough compared to the silky green grass grown in the forest of my childhood home. Frustrated, I grabbed the jacket that was slung across the back of my chair. Jabbing my arms into the arm holes I reached for my keys and phone and shoved them into my jacket pocket. Walking swiftly through the desks littered around the large precinct I made it to the front doors without anybody stopping to talk to me. Changing my mind about driving anywhere, I set out to walk around the block. I was feeling restless and kind of useless. I had been trying to find the missing children that Detective Viv and shown me

CHAPTER NINE

in that file months ago at the restaurant. I didn't remember the cases with John being this troubling. I was feeling like something was holding me back, there was a virtual wall between my brain and the ability to communicate with the children in the file. I knew they were in a dark place but they couldn't hear vehicles driving or people talking or give me any land markers. I hadn't been sleeping well, I was being woken up by nightmares and when I tried to figure out what they meant it was like trying to pin down jello. The thoughts just slipped out of my mind. My frustration would grow when I had a flash of a dream and then it disappeared. Is this how normal people feel about their dreams, I wondered. I was going stir crazy in the brick building full of police officers. They were like peacocks strutting around trying to be better than each other. I realized I missed the quiet of the reserve. The tall trees, the creek, the dogs which wandered about looking for a free meal. The family members who were happy to see me and who wanted to talk to me not bark orders at me like I was a soldier. Without realizing where I was headed I noticed I had walked to a known Indian hospital, now closed, it was a hotspot for tuberculosis back in the 1940's. It is enclosed in a metal fence but the building still stands. The dark windows looking out onto

CHAPTER NINE

the city surrounding it. There were so many unknown deaths from this place. Little children never knowing their families but sent here to be raised until they died from tuberculosis. I had heard many horror stories but I had also heard that the "Indians" who were brought here liked the feeling of belonging. They liked that if they were sick and needed to be away from their homes that the people here were also missing their families and they would bond over the crafts they were able to do. Some of the older patients would tell stories from their homes and share with the children who gathered around them. It seemed that the government would go out of their way to collect the patients from the northern reservations but upon their deaths they would just bury them in a collective graveyard not far from the hospital. Their graves, mostly unmarked, except the ones who would claim a Protestant or Catholic deity were remembered in a log book kept by the church. How many were long gone, buried without words to carry them on to their final journey. Me heart aches and I feel the anger well up in my chest. The damage done, the families torn apart, the gaping hole in our society which could have been filled with a giant group of Indigenous Peoples willing to share their history and stories and simple way of life. My eyes wandered over the big

CHAPTER NINE

empty building. Placing my hands on the wire fence, I close my eyes and asked Creator to watch over the missing and help them home, to help heal the ones who had been able to leave the hospital and go to their families and to all the health professionals who had thought they could help the Indians to find peace. I breath in a big breath and release it and feel the energy inside me replaced with calm. I need the calm. I think of the towering trees at my home, the tinkling of the stream. My head clears and I release my grip on the fence. How am I going to find the missing children that detective Viv needs me to help with. I continue walking and wonder about the person, the monster, who had taken the children. What kind of motive, what were any similarities between the victims. Then like a dam busting my thoughts align with each other. There is no connection between the children but what of the connection with the person responsible. I think about what I had been reading, the similarities, the location. How had the police not noticed the location, the person they all knew. I pulled out my cell phone and dialed Detective Viv.

"It's Mark, I'm on my way back to the precinct." I hastily spoke into the phone when the Detective answered. "I have a theory we haven't gone

CHAPTER NINE

over. Be there in 20 mins" I hung up the phone without waiting for an answer and smiled for the first time in weeks.

My eyes looked up again at the old abandoned Indian hospital. Faces looked out at me, smiling and looking back over their shoulders, some waved as they disappeared others just left. I said good bye to the ones who got through to me and lifted my hand in a final farewell to the sweet children who vanished. My steps a little lighter my head held high I began walking back to the police precinct. My thoughts were racing a mile a minute, I wanted to share my thoughts with Elder John but he wasn't around anymore.

In a few minutes I was taking the front stairs two at a time in my rush to get to the detective and share with her.

CHAPTER TEN

Swinging the doors wide open I race towards my desk in the back of the precinct, and I see the beautiful Detective sitting on the edge of my desk looking at my photo of John. My mind wanders for a moment, taking in her thoughtful smile, I can see the vein throbbing in her temple…that means she is holding her energy in. Waiting impatiently to see me and spring her energy my way. I appreciate the knowledge and slow to a walk, waiting for her to acknowledge my presence. As if sensing my arrival, Detective Viv turns her head towards me and slowly rises from my desk. Her lips curve up in a small smile but her eyes…they look at me like we have won the lottery. Sensing something more I return her smile and ask,

"What have I missed in the last hour Detective?" I slowly move around my desk and sit in my chair.

"We got him" her smile widens and her eyes sparkle. Coming to the desk she grabs me off the chair and hugs me tight. "We got the son of a

CHAPTER TEN

bitch who hurt them all." Letting me go she grabs the thick file from my active case files. She opens it up and looks at all the pictures of the children, her eyes watery she hands me the photos and says, "please, lets take them home"

I look at the pictures in her hand, the smiling pictures, the whole pictures, taking them in my hand I look at each one individually, my vision blurs suddenly and the little red haired boy is speaking to me,

"Thank you Mark! I get to go home and say goodbye to my mom and dad and my sister, they cry a lot but maybe they can stop now. Will you tell them I love them and I am happy to be with Creator now?"

Not thinking, I nod my head in the affirmative and answer out loud,

"Yes, I will let them know"

"Ok I will meet you there!" The little boy hollers before he leaves me.

CHAPTER TEN

Vision clearing, I see Detective Viv looking at me with quizzical eyes, her head cocked in thought. "Having a different conversation than the one with me?" She asks.

"Not different, just another conversation." I reply

"Ok" she responds "so if your done with that conversation, could we do some paperwork and make some phone calls to meet with the parents. If it was me I would want to know every detail and what the process is now for the families."

"Sure" I reply "lets get to finishing this case, I think I need a little holiday."

Sitting at the desk next to mine the Detective smiles a little and takes one of the folders. Turning on the computer she finds the files for this case and begins typing in the final findings. I take another file and begin the process myself, I feel the Detective clear her mind, was that a picture of me in there? I smile to myself. I remember the day 6 months earlier, I

CHAPTER TEN

had been returning to the city from my 48 hour trip to my home reservation.

I was so eager to get to work, find the children on this missing persons case which had unfortunately turned into a homicide case and then we linked it to a serial killer case which had been stale for about ten years. The cute detective and I had worked long hours and talked about everything, without knowing it we began to finish each other's sentences, when someone yelled out at us across the precinct we both looked up and answered them simultaneously. We ate breakfast, lunch and had dinner almost everyday together. I told her about Elder John and she said she had met him a couple times in passing but hadn't really worked with him on a case. She knew I missed him terribly. We were slowly becoming a couple not just working partners. The evil we had to witness and sort through to finish the case was hard. We leaned on each other when we needed to and we went to separate and couples counselling. It seemed to help get us through the rough days. We continuously had to update the five families of the case we had before us. They were sad, scared, angry. All the feelings overlapping each other and they only really had us to lash

CHAPTER TEN

out at. We had to figure this out. We had to complete this nightmare so the families could continue on with their lives. They were all waiting for their child to be found alive or dead. I knew they were gone but I couldn't tell them this without proof, it was frustrating. One day at a time we would work together and finish this. I was grateful to have this wonderful person in my life.

Blinking my eyes I look over at the detective working on her computer she was concentrating on the screen in front of her. So I put my head down and begin my own work, pushing all thoughts of her out, I begin my own typing.

CHAPTER ELEVEN

The lights off on the patrol car, Detective Viv and I arrive at a small suburban house along the river valley. The streets are lined with tall trees and sidewalks where children and adults are walking their dogs on leashes or biking lazily along the dark pavement enjoying the minutes before dark. The street lights waiting to be turned on, the sun casting long shadows along the road. It is a nice quiet older subdivision. A place to raise a family, have bbq dinners on backyard patios, make real friends with your neighbours. Parking along the road I notice everyone looking at us as we open the doors and walk up the front drive. Some people just turn their heads and keep on with their activity but others slow their walking, stopping to pet their animals, or tie a shoe or get out their phones to make a call. I hear Detective Viv, let out a small breath and say what sounds like a little prayer under her breath. I brush my shoulder to hers so she can feel a connection to me and know that I feel the same as she does while we have to deliver this tragic news to this little family. Running her damp palms along her pants she lifts her hand to press the doorbell and we wait just seconds before the door opens to a pretty red haired lady about 30

CHAPTER TWELVE

years old. On closer inspection of her face I notice the lines around her puffy eyes, and the lips that quiver as she notices us. She opens the screen door and asks us to come in and have a seat in her living room. There are framed pictures scattered on every surface, the little red haired boy and a young pretty girl laughing in every frame. My heart squeezes at the injustice. A life stolen, a family shattered, for no sensical reason. I realize that Detective Viv is asking for the woman's husband to join us and he shortly enters the room and takes a seat beside his wife and gently holds her hand in his. Eyes downcast they listen as Detective Viv introduces me and explains where we are the investigation in searching for their little boy, his name is Tyler. She quietly and in precise words explains that we have found Tyler and the other children. The mom weeps silently, dad just looks at us and closes his eyes. Silent tears fall from the corners of his eyes. I rise and grab the box of tissues closest to me and place them in his hand. The telephone rings but no one rises to answer it and then there is silence. The family can start to mourn. The Detective assures the parents that we are continuing on with the investigation and will let them know of any advancements. She lets them know their little boy is at the coroners office and they can arrange to see him and gives them the coroners

CHAPTER TWELVE

business card. She also advises them to call a funeral home and they will help with all matters. The mom, with her head still head bowed and crying silently nods her head and squeezes her husbands hand. He briefly lets her had go and rises, we follow him to the door, he shakes our hand and impulsively I grab him in a quick tight hug.

I whisper in his ear, "Tyler is safe in Creators arms now, he has peace and wishes the same for the rest of you."

"Thank you" he whispers back

The Detective and I head back to the car in silence. Looking back I see Tyler staring at us from the living room window waving goodbye. His big blue eyes twinkle and he disappears.

We head back to the precinct in silence the radio crackling with police chatter. Dropping the cruiser in the parking spot at the police compound we enter the building by the back door, the fluorescent lights making me blink my eyes a couple times their low hum vibrating off the cold stone walls. Finding our way to the front office we let the dispatcher know we

CHAPTER TWELVE

are back and are heading home for the night. Going to our desks we turn off the computers and straighten our desks, putting the coffee cups in the sink so the cleaning crew can wash them up. The detective has to do one more step before we leave and that is to check in her firearm with the cage. Once she has done that and signed her name and badge number on the digital form we head out the door to our personal vehicles. We haven't spoken a word since we left Tyler's house. We walk to her car first and with her hand on the door handle she looks at me with quiet sad eyes. Gently I lay my hand on hers and remove it from her car door, holding it lightly I lead her to my car and open the door for her to slip in. She does, quietly, elegantly and lets my hand go as I close the door and walk around to the driver side and just as quietly I slip in behind the wheel and push the start button. The motor hums quietly and the air conditioner starts softly blowing cool air in to the vehicle. Backing the car up we leave the parking space and drive around the city for a couple hours. Viv is quiet for the first half hour then she quietly speaks of her family. They are not perfect but caring. Lucky she had her family for years to support her decisions or challenge the hard choices she had made. But always they were there, the family we went to see tonight would never know the

CHAPTER TWELVE

promise that young Tyler had. Nor any of the families we had to go see tomorrow. The case was closing, the time to pick up the predator was nearing. There were eyes on him so that nobody else would be harmed but the paperwork needed to be complete before continuing on. We didn't want him to be let out on a technicality that could have been prevented with all our paperwork being done properly. Nothing for us to do tonight though. Viv lets her hand softly cover mine and we head to my place.

Opening the underground parking I find my spot and make sure nothing is amiss. Opening the passenger door and helping her out of the car we walk holding hands to the elevator that would take us soundlessly up to the penthouse floor. I hear her soft gasp as the doors open to my apartment, and she quickly turns her head in my direction. I was looking at her and not the room so I didn't miss the dilating of her pupils as her gaze found mine. I remove my light jacket and hang it up in the hall closet. She chuckles softly shaking her head a bit and smiles. Turning her gently I remove her jacket and hang it up beside mine. Gesturing her in the direction of the comfy leather couch while I go to the fridge for some

CHAPTER TWELVE

cold wine, some cheese, crackers and fruit for a small charcuterie board. Pouring two glasses of wine I set one on the kitchen island counter and as I come around it to give her her glass she stands up and comes to sit at the counter. I place her wine on the gleaming white marble top and smile. She sips and I go turn on some jazz music. It helps with the quiet. She watches as I cut fruit and meat into bite sized pieces. The cheese cut into perfect cubes. A bit of pickled onions and a couple pickled asparagus spears a bit of sourdough bread cubed as well. I open the cupboards and find some crackers to place on the board as well. It looks good. A perfect little snack after such an emotional day. As I chop and arrange our charcuterie board I ask her some pointed questions about her family while she in turn tries to get answers about me. I know she is curious about my home and my vehicles. I know I haven't been as open and sharing with her as she has been with me. I haven't shared all the details of my trip back to the residential school or my forty eight hour trip to my home reservation. Maybe I will explain all that tonight or maybe wait for another day. We talk late into the night. Finally with weary eyes we head to bed. The day had been an exhausting one, emotionally. Sometimes, it is very hard to leave the work at work. Holding my hand she guides me to the

CHAPTER TWELVE

bedroom, opens the door and as I turn on the light, she turns towards me and reaches out to turn the light off. We fall into the plush king sized bed fully clothed and fall asleep holding hands.

CHAPTER TWELVE

The sun streaming into the patio doors awakens me, that's odd, I usually close all the blinds so it stays dark in the bedroom. I look towards the patio and notice the doors are wide open. The last evening comes roaring into focus, Vivian is here, with me. Laughing I tell myself we actually had a sleep over. Where we slept. Humming I get up and go to the balcony, the sun is shining and I see her looking over the edge, her hair down blowing in the wind. She looks up and over at me a wide smile on her lips, she looks like a goddess the sun making her skin glitter. I could imagine us like this for years to come. Vivian radiant in the morning sun, my mind free of nighttime cobwebs. I haven't felt this refreshed after a sleep in so long.

"Good morning Mark, this is like paradise" she says to me

"You look nice, good morning Vivian." I respond to her and smile. A nice relaxed smile. "Would you like breakfast and coffee" I ask her. Knowing I would cook for her everyday of our lives.

CHAPTER TWELVE

Sensing a shift in the mood she looks at the sky and down below and back to me, "I would like a shower first if that's ok with you"

"Of course" I reply, " there are extra towels in the hall closet."

She walks by me and heads to the closet to gather towels and comes back in the room and heads to my master bathroom.

"You coming?" She asked me with a laugh

"Yes, I am" I answer back with a laugh

A while later as the water starts running cold we step out of the shower and dry each other off, sensing her dilemma I offer to drive her to her house to get some clean clothes before we head into work. She accepts and I hand her some sweat pants and a t-shirt to wear in the meantime. She heads to the kitchen to make coffee and search for some breakfast while I dress and get ready for another day of work. In about 3 minutes the smell of bacon wafts through the air making my mouth water.

CHAPTER TWELVE

Finishing my hair I step out of the master bath and walk across the room to close the balcony doors, drawing the blinds closed and the room is cool and dark again. Kind of a metaphor for my life I think, just closing the doors and drawing the blinds closed like closing out the world and retreating back to my dark life. Then I smell coffee wrestling with the delicious smell of bacon and eggs and I smile. Maybe I don't need the quiet darkness, maybe I just need Vivian who brings light and laughter and wonderful smells. Would she feel the same as me, I wonder. I remember her bright smile as I watches her on the balcony earlier. Her quiet strength and her moral compass always set on compassion and understanding. We belong together I know it in my soul. Smiling I enter the kitchen and offer to butter the toast.

We enjoy a light, banter filled, quick breakfast and quickly clean up the kitchen and it is soon back to its gleaming white state. I watch as Vivian walks to the closet to retrieve her jacket I think that the light leaves with her even if the counters are brilliantly white. I walk towards her and smile as I get my light jacket from the closet and grab my keys from the hall table. I check to make sure I have my wallet and phone and I gently

CHAPTER TWELVE

close the door behind us as we wait for the elevator to return us to the garage level and all the harsh reality that we have avoided the last 12 hours. I enjoy this closeness, how we can be together and be quiet and just enjoy the feelings. Once we exit the elevator, the Detective heads towards the car I was driving yesterday and I gently grab her hand and steer her towards another, she looks at me and raises one of her eyebrows in question and I laugh, a little laugh, a happy laugh. We are going to drive the Escalade today, a nice smooth ride. I can see the detective driving this around, she's so delicate and this monster of a machine would make her feel ten feet tall. In contrast to most of my other vehicles this sleek black machine gleams when the sunlight hits it. The windows are darkened with tint and the seats are leather and hand stitched. I help Vivian into the truck and walk around to the driver side. I notice Vivian has her seatbelt on already and her hands are clasped tightly in her lap, the workday and all its ugliness has started. I mourn our idyllic morning already. Turning on the stereo I find a nice light pop station and try to smile. Exiting the garage we turn onto the busy morning traffic streets and merge with hundreds of others trying to get to work on time. I make idle

CHAPTER TWELVE

conversation, ask Vivian if she could go to dinner with me at the end of the day, she looks at me with sadness and longing in her eyes.

"Dinner sounds nice, but lets see how the day plays out before we make any plans ok?" She asks me.

"Ok" I reply

I drive to her house, a quiet, brick structure. The grass is mowed and green, there's a tall tree and hedges dividing her property from the neighbours. No flowers but I can understand that with her hectic work hours. Pulling into the driveway, she undoes her seatbelt and tells me she will be right back. I watch her run up the stairs and unlock and open her front door. She emerges just minutes later wearing her black suit and black shoes her hair pinned up tightly. I remember how it was splayed across my pillow last night as I fell asleep holding her hand and I smile. She opens the door and gives me back my sweats and t-shirt and thanks me for letting her borrow them.

CHAPTER TWELVE

On the drive to the precinct Vivian tells me her plan for the day, which households she will visit, she tells me the names of the children and their parents even their siblings. She knows this case inside and out and I know it must be eating at her that these lives were taken. How long did she say she had been in this division? It must be awhile, how can humanity and kindness win out over this kind of everyday trauma. At least I had the privilege of talking with those that were leaving, I had the chance to say goodby to them and help them with their journey. All Viv has is a grieving family, endless conversations on how, why, where, when. Sometimes I knew she didn't have the answers and it frustrated her and it hurt the families who needed answers where there weren't any. Would she come away with me for a holiday when this was completed? I wondered at how many other cases she had on her desk were they almost finished? Could she leave? Would she want to? A million other little questions hummed through my brain as I drove into the police parking compound. Vivian turned to me and smiled her little smile.

"Thank you for staying with me yesterday, it helps to have you around. It is going to be a busy long day and if I can get a break would

CHAPTER TWELVE

you walk with me? I go to the little café down a couple blocks and get a coffee and breathe." Vivians eyes were troubled already and I knew my answer in an instant.

"Of course, just text or call me if I'm not in the office, I will be close by." Finding my parking spot I turn the truck off and jump out and go around to open the door but Vivian is already standing outside, hands in her pockets, staring at the building, back ramrod straight. It's her officer pose, I've seen it a few times when she is trying to compose her feelings, turning them off I suppose. It's her way of getting through the day, I sympathize and wonder how I would do it if I had to turn off my emotions as I had had to do when I was younger, retreating into the dark corners of my mind. Shaking my head I stop, I didn't have to go there anymore. The voices are welcomed in my mind now, encouraged. The chance, the privilege I have to converse with, to help those continue on their final journey, I would never shut those voices our again. I am humbled to be the one to help them through whatever is needed of me.

CHAPTER TWELVE

Vivian starts the conversation first, "Ok lets get this finished, letting these families know what has happened is important. Let them begin to grieve, begin to heal. We have done our job and now we need to let it go. Tonight we will let it go."

It's like a little pep talk to get her through the day. I have heard her say little things like that every morning for months. I appreciated her way of putting on her work "armour" and I certainly appreciated how she took it off at night when her shift was done. I admired it actually. The way she could try live her life normally when she held so many lives in her hands. It must be something learned in counselling. I had planned to ask her to marry me tonight, she was my soulmate. Vivian would say yes, she had to. We belonged together, this I new without a doubt in my mind. We had a long time to learn everything about each other. I had to introduce her to my family. I smiled thinking how my sister would love her. And little Markie would have another auntie. Shaking my head I thought to myself just get through this day and tonight I will have my answer.

CHAPTER TWELVE

Vivian looks at me gives a little nod and heads inside. The office is already noisy, radios crackling in the background, some laughing between the officers just starting their shifts. I realize this is their job, its important, it can be life or death every single shift. I nod to some of the officers who acknowledge us as we walk by, stopping to speak to one who had a few questions regarding another case. I assured him I would be on it as soon as the current case is closed. Maybe a holiday or honeymoon is out of the question.

By the time I reach my desk I see that Detective Vivian is already on the phone a thick file in front of her. I sit at my desk and turn on the computer screen. Slowly it buzzes and blue screen comes on it takes a few seconds before the bold black writing comes on and I log in and see what sort of emails I have waiting for me today. Before I know it its coffee time and I look around for the detective, she's not at her desk. I look at my phone and see a text. It's from her and reads,

be back soon just heading to family to notify of case findings. See you at coffee.

I text back quickly and reply that its coffee time now.

Immediately I receive a text back,

CHAPTER TWELVE

I'm at the coffee shop waiting for you.

Smiling I gather up my light jacket, phone and keys. I log off my computer and head out the front door deciding to walk to the coffee shop. As I approach the coffee shop I look inside the window. I see her in her black suit. She looks tired, we need a break.

Opening the door she looks up at me and smiles. A gentle smile, it warms my heart a little more. There is a coffee cup filled and mixed with sugar already when I sit down. I slowly take a sip. It's pretty good. The waitress walks over as I put the cup down and asks if I would like anything else. I tell her no thank you and let her know the coffee is perfect. She smiles at me and walks away to help her next customer.

Talking softly to Viv, I ask how her day has been so far. Her sad eyes look at me and I know the visits she has had to do this morning have taken their toll on her.

We talk about how the team had descended on to the man responsible for tearing these families apart. He had been picked up at 5 am. Before

CHAPTER TWELVE

he could start his day. They had found numerous disturbing things in his house. He had made a home, he felt safe. He had a video set room so he could take film of the things he had done. The room had cement floors, and yellow wallpaper. He had video tapes going back twenty years. All the horror this man had brought, he would never see daylight again. If the inmates didn't rip him apart, he would be behind bars a long time. A monster hiding in sheep's clothing. Like the priests, nuns and the Catholic Church had done for years. This man had hid behind a physicians coat. A pediatrician. A trusted medical person. The families had placed their children right in his path without knowing his true nature. How had this happened, how did our society just trust in people. Who decided that these people were to be given control over our lives. I was shocked when I had learned this but maybe there was a reason, there had to be, why this monster was the way he was. What had happened to him, I would not feel sorry for him but I knew he must have had some horror, or some brain imbalance some drug addiction something had to have made him into the person he was today.

CHAPTER TWELVE

We finish our conversation and our coffee. Together we leave the building walking towards her car. I get into the passenger seat and do up my seatbelt. Waiting for Viv to get in and head back to the police precinct.

Before we enter the red brick building the detective looks over at me and smiles. She takes a breath and blows it out. Undoes her seatbelt and reaches in to her pocket. In her hand is a single gold band. Elegant, slim, timeless. She takes my hand and looks me in the eyes.

"Mark, we have been through so much this past year, we fit together so well, you are my rock when I need you to be. You have so much compassion and are so thoughtful to everyone who you meet. Everyday I look forward to talking with you and sharing my thoughts, you are so understanding. It is what I love about you the most." She pauses a minute.

She loves me, I think to myself. We belong together.

"I have waited for you for so long, would you marry me" she asks me with a question mark

CHAPTER TWELVE

"Of course I will" I smile at her as she places my gold band on my finger and reaches into her other pocket for a matching band for herself. I gently take it and place it on her finger and raise her hand to my lips and kiss it. I will love and care for her forever and maybe even longer.

It's my last action, my last thought

Suddenly I am weak, finding trouble to breathe, I look at my hands, I am in the dark, I smell the decades old urine stained mattress. My body smells. My hair is rough and short. I know where I am. Silently I cry. My hands bunched into tiny fists of rage and regret. Why me, why me, why now? I just want to go home, I want to live. I know I can have a life if I am just able to try. My body shivers, I'm kneeling on the floor, my hands clasped in prayer. My last breath leaves me in quiet, alone, and in the dark. I am there for 3 days before my body is found. The older boys wrap me in canvas and tie yellow rope abound my feet so they stay together. Unceremoniously I am put into a hole, there are others there, we are all dead. None of us will ever go home, grow up or have families of our own.

CHAPTER TWELVE

I see all this happen. I am floating above the ground.

Little Mary comes to stand beside me and she puts her hand in mine and says, "the time will come. They will find us and bring us home. For now do you want to come play with us?"

I look at her and blink my eyes, I am fourteen years old. I have been here for half of my life, abused for half of my life. I look at little Mary, eyes so wise, younger but so much wiser. I shake my head and tell her I have a journey to do and I will come back to her. Nodding her head, she squeezes my hand and disappears.

Vaguely I remember an older lady, dark hair, kind eyes, dressed as a police officer. My little heart contracts. This was the life I should have had, with her. I was going to be happy, content I was going to have cars and trucks. Rapid flashes of a life I should have had, pictures of gleaming white counters and tall trees with silky green grass tickling underfoot. Golden bands on our fingers, a beautiful brown eyed lady dressed in white

CHAPTER TWELVE

waiting for me by a river. Bundles of fish caught in my net. Finally, two children, raven black hair and big brown eyes, skin touched by the sun a golden brown. A laughing little girl and a bashful little boy. My children. My beautiful children. A happy life, one I should have had but instead I am here…waiting.

Come find us! I silently scream

I'm not ready

Made in the USA
Columbia, SC
04 August 2021